THE GHOSTS OF
THE PAST

Luigi Pascal Rondanini

Independent

English Version ISBN: 979-8-8707-9801-1
English Version ASIN: B0CPLLSD51

Italian Version EAN: 978-8-8334-3643-2
Italian Version ISBN: 88-3343-643-8
Italian Version Publisher: LFA Publisher, Naples (IT)

Cover design by: Luigi Pascal Rondanini
Printed in the United Kingdom

To my father, Pasquale.

I love you.

Your son

CONTENTS

FOREWORD

This work is the English translation of the Italian original "I Fantasmi del Passato" published by LFA Publisher in Naples, Italy. While the key plot events and character development have been faithfully adapted for the English version, some dialogue has necessarily been modified due to the challenges of translating certain authentic Neapolitan expressions into English. Regional colloquialisms unique to southern Italy simply do not carry over directly.

Additionally, in consideration of an English speaking readership's sensibilities, some of the coarser language and insulting interjections repeatedly used in the Italian version have been toned down or omitted. Swear words and crude references that may be common in casual conversation among native Neapolitan speakers come across as jarringly abrasive when translated. Thus, selective editing of vulgarities was required for the English adaptation.

That said, the fundamental essence of the conversation and complex decades-long relationship between childhood friends Antonio and Giorgio remains intact. All major revelations, and the bittersweet ultimate redemption between the flawed characters are authentically preserved.

Please enjoy this English rendition of "I Fantasmi del Passato" which aims to capture the spirit of the Italian original while smoothing its translation for an English literary audience.

The author.

ACT ONE

(In a bar on the eastern outskirts of Naples, a middle-aged man enters, recognising someone, an old acquaintance)

Antonio: Is that you? Giorgio, how are you?

(The acquaintance, similar age, turns around calmly)

Giorgio: Hello Anto'. Yes, it's me. Are you okay?

A: Well, yes, everything is fine. Are you on vacation?

G: I came to see my dad. I took the kids to visit their relatives and grandpa, who is alone now. You heard about my mother.

A: I called Massimino when I heard about her passing away. You were also there, but you had gone out for a moment. I told your brother to let you know about my call and left him my number in case you wanted to hear from me.

G: You'll have to excuse me, but it hadn't been an easy few days. Do you know how it is?

(Giorgio looks around, embarrassed).

A: Of course. How long are you staying in Naples?

G: I'm leaving tomorrow. Unfortunately, I have to go back to work early; with the separation drama and my father alone in Naples, I'm going back and forth very often. How about you?

(Antonio approaches smilingly).

A: I arrived last night and I'll be leaving on Sunday. Three or four days, touch and go. I have to see the producer of the film they are going to make out of my book. The director should also be there; they want to show me the list of actors to see if they fit as characters. I mean, now and then, I'm also in Naples for business. Do you want a coffee? Or anything?

G: Sure, yes, let's go for a coffee.

(They approach the counter)

A: Oreste, two coffees, please.

G: You are also separated, aren't you? How are the children?

A: I am separated and remarried. One child with the first and one with the second. Hoping it will be better this time. I picked an Italian wife this time.

G: Good luck with the Italians.

A: Of course, it's not a walk in the park, as you can imagine, but it could be worse. And about the children's question... How are they? Hmmm, they're fine, I suppose. Children are very judgmental. It matters little whether you do good or bad; if you do bad to do them well, they're always there to have a go at you. I mean, of all professions, parenting is the most difficult one. I have succeeded in everything, but being a father is not my forte. On the other hand, have you been separated for a long time?

(Giorgio responds almost hesitantly)

G: It must be two years now.

A: I was shocked when I heard it. Maybe I thought that I was the only one that could divorce. But it seemed so strange; you were together for a long time. The children? How did they take it?

G: Unfortunately, that happened, but I've come to terms with it and spent a lot of time with the guys. I have to say that being home a lot has helped to create a good relationship with them; apart from when we had to announce, suddenly, that we were breaking up, it didn't go that badly.

A: I'm glad to hear that. How is your father? I saw him the last time I was here. He's old and talks a lot about your mother.

G: Yes, it's not entirely sane up there.

(Giorgio signals with his hand by rotating his finger several times at temple level)

A: Well, he's in his nineties now, right?

G: Ninety-two, to be precise.

A: Well...not bad. You know you and I haven't seen each other since 1992 and haven't spoken to each other since 2000.

G: No, we saw each other after 2000. You're mistaken.

A: No, I was in Milan on business. I called you, and you said you couldn't meet me. Don't you remember?

G: Not really. We saw each other later, though.

A: Impossible, because after you told me you couldn't even have coffee in the morning, it was a Sunday, as you had friends for dinner in the evening, I didn't contact you again.

G: Strange, I really don't remember.

(Antonio drinks the coffee, forging a grimace)

A: Thanks for the coffee, Oreste, always excellent

G: Do you really like it?

(Antonio laughs)

A: No, it sucks, like in the old days.

(Antonio laughs with gusto)

(Moment of silence between the two)

G: I saw that you had a good career, although I thought you would be a professional politician.

A: No, I have always liked politics, but being a radical at my core, I find it difficult to settle with any political party and say yes to all compromises. I have always been unaccustomed to compromises. Otherwise, I am not complaining. I did all the jobs I wanted and got recognition in every field.

G: What do you call yourself today? A writer, a communicator, an influencer?

A: No, no, influencer, just no. I leave that to those who have no craft. I like to say what I think and don't care who agrees and who doesn't. Then, maybe you know I don't have any online presence. I don't have Facebook, Instagram, TikTok. In one sentence: I don't give a shit about social media.

G: I feel like I read about you everywhere. Occasionally, your name pops up on one side or the other. I once searched online, and you appeared where people talked about finance, politics, and books. You may not have a page or profile; however, you are everywhere.

A: And why were you looking for me?

G: No reason, really.

A: Not so you could contact me, I guess. I also tried to track you online, but you don't exist.

G: No, I never wanted to have a public showcase. I'm not like you. Then, you have no reason to have your own social media presence; other people do it to promote you. At every opportunity, you pop up.

(Antonio gets embarrassed)

A: Well, but I don't write about myself. Other people do. And not always in a positive way, unsurprisingly. For someone who has been abroad all his life, Italians seem more interested in me than English people.

G: That's true, you also write in English. I found a few articles and even interviews where you talk about English politics.

A: They will be old articles when the Liberal Democratic Party made me run for a seat where I could not win. They put me there not to burn any good candidate. You know the electoral system in Britain is different than in Italy.

G: For the better, I hope.

A: Usually, you vote against the favourite rather than for your own candidate. So, being in a constituency where my party had no chance of winning made me the sacrificial victim. Ultimately, it went better than I thought, and I picked up a lot more votes than the main opposition candidate, but I came second, so I was out.

G: Whatever, come on. Good though.

A: They then wanted me to run for a by-election two years later somewhere else, but I had too many commitments, and English politics sucks more than Italian, so I said no. But I have to admit that that experience helped me in my career. I still get invited to various shows, both on radio and TV, to talk about politics.

G: But so you are British now? And why didn't you ever run with the socialists?

A: Yes, I've been British for over 30 years, and no, Labour is not what it used to be. It's like the Italian communists when we were young. Not for me, thanks. The Liberal Democrats are similar to the Italian radicals of the old days, so I get along well with them.

G: Yes, I remember you were both socialist and radical.

A: Now I'm really nothing. I get involved in the things I like and the social causes I care about. Anyway, this coffee really sucks.

(Puts down the cup on the counter).

G: Do you remember when we made deliveries for Don Salvatore, Oreste's dad?

A: Right! We used to spit in it when we knew they wouldn't give us the tip!

(They both laugh)

G: What a laugh. True.

A: You know what I was thinking a while ago? When I see movies or read books about friends meeting after a long time, they remember the mischief. I don't think you and I have ever done any. In fact, even in my books, I find it hard to tell about the mischiefs of my younger characters.

G: And why would that be? With the imagination you have, it shouldn't be that difficult.

A: Maybe because of what I was saying earlier. I don't have a story of mischief that I feel is my own and writing about the sassing and running to the hospital, the tortures, and the sewer water balloons don't seem so educational or enlightening. Am I wrong?

G: You are not wrong. We were the only ones not being streetwise around here. You with the constant party engagements, me always chasing girls.

A: You destroyed me! You are telling me that I was a geek who didn't give a shit about women.

G: Actually, it was me who should be ashamed, as girls were the only thing I ever thought about

A: So true. Despite everything, we had a fun time. It was a good youth. It was such a long time ago... We are older than our parents then. It's scary just thinking about it.

(A gentleman enters and greets Giorgio)

G: Good morning, good morning.

A: Who is he? I don't know him.

G. He's my nephew's father-in-law, Massimino's elder son.

A: Never seen him.

G: They're from the area but have never frequented our buildings. Good people.

A: I'm glad to hear that. Listen, at lunchtime, what are you doing? You don't happen to want to go for a bite together?

G: Unfortunately, I'm having lunch with the kids at my sister's, Susanna's, today. So I can't. But maybe next time.

A: Yes, next time, in 30 years. At my or your funeral.

G: Eh, I guess so. Never put a limit on providence. I am curious: why don't you use your name when writing?

A: It's an old story.

(Pause for reflection).

A: When I wrote the first book, I worked with a news agency that did not allow contributors to write independently. So, I chose a pen name to publish, regardless.

G: Neapolitan inside. Nice cheater.

A: As time passed, I continued using the same name rather than my own. It seems like a watershed between Antonio Russo of the old days and Pascal de Napoli today.

G: But Pascal is written the Spanish way, not in Italian, so why not Pasquale?

A: Because I never liked the letter Q. Pascal can be read the Neapolitan or the English way. It suited me since my first books were in English.

G: I have to say that I still find it incredible to think that someone born here, raised here, is now English and writes in English. Very strange.

A: For someone who wanted to be Swedish, that's not bad.

(Antonio thinks of something. Then he remembers what he wanted to say.)

A: How is it that Lello Arena used to say? You know where you are born but don't know where you die...

G: True. Me too, who knows where the hell I am going to perish.

A: If it were possible to know, one would do the impossible to never go there.

G: So the de Napoli is a tribute to Naples, or else?

A: To pay homage to my city, my favourite football team, but especially to the cultural imprint that remains intact, even though I live in London.

G: For the series, anything goes, but not being Italian.

(Antonio smiles)

A: You liked Sweden, didn't you? You studied Swedish at

university and, if I'm not mistaken, spent six months there before the summer in Montesilvano. Do, or did you consider yourself Swedish?

G: No. Not at all.

A: There you go; the same thing applies to me. I like all of Italy, from the North to the South, but I don't consider myself Italian. Also, I should have a passport, and I don't have one to be Italian. I left Naples when I was 18 and moved abroad when I was 21. Now, I am almost 60. You do the math a bit and determine what makes more sense.

G: Oikophobe! Just kidding. I see what you mean. The Neo-Bourbons occasionally mention you.

A: Fuck them. I have never supported them. Neither openly nor privately. Borbonia doesn't suit me either. Who wants to have Lucania as part of a country? Nobody! The nice Parthenopean Republic, at most, includes the lands now in Ciociaria. If Rome wants to join us, they are welcome.

(Laughs amused, Antonio)

G: I have different experiences with the Lucani. I always got along well, but everyone has experiences, so let's be it. You were saying they are making a movie from one of your books?

A: Yes. The book is not yet published. It's coming out after the movie. The publisher said doing it like that for this book is better. I honestly don't give a damn. I like writing. In fact, if it hadn't turned out who Pascal de Napoli was, it would have been better. Still, unfortunately, with that plagiarism issue, I couldn't keep it a secret.

G: What plagiarism? I didn't know.

A: About fifteen years ago, I had written a book they later found around various sites. It was written by a chap calling himself

Pascual de Napoles. He didn't even have the imagination to choose another name, this gentleman from Barcelona. He copied the book, changed the names, and translated everything into Catalan.

G: What a story...

A: The book had been published by a Spanish company, and when the English version arrived in London, my publisher pointed it out to me. So we sued, and at that point, I had to jump out to prove that my book, Vanished Echoes, had been plagiarised.

G: I got it. And is it possible to know who the actors are in this new film, or is it a secret?

A: Actually, I don't know either. In the movie, people propose two or three actors for each role. We'll see. I'll let you know who they are, but the author doesn't decide. They do it out of courtesy.

(Antonio looks toward a small room at the side of the bar counter. The light is off, and no one is there.)

A: Whatever. I have an idea. Maybe we can get a deck of cards and play a game of tressette? What do you say? Like in the old days?

G: No, thank you. Tressette... I can't even remember how to play it anymore.

A: Shall we play the losers' version of it? Maybe you're good at losing!

G: Yeah, yeah, keep taking the piss. After ten minutes of poker, you were the one who had already lost all your money.

A: But there was a reason.

G: Let's hear it...

(Antonio touches his goatee and pretends to think).

A: I was not too fond of poker, but because you and the others liked it, I used to lose what little I had right away so you wouldn't bust my balls.

(Giorgio jerks as if he's had a brilliant idea).

G: Unbelievable! After so many years, I know why the genius from Naples couldn't last ten minutes at poker. And I thought you were thick.

(Both laugh)

A: Actually, the dullard is you who still doesn't understand, even today, how come I was teaching you the tricks to bluff at poker, and you were winning while I wasn't.

G: So you were rooting for me.

A: Let's say I was coaching you for free.

G: And even when it came to women, you weren't after anyone because you were too busy coaching me?

A: Well, brother, if you'll allow me to say so, you had horrible tastes. From Maddalena to Rosanna to the "Swede", they were one shittier than the other; however, you only needed to dump the load.

(Giorgio lowers his gaze with embarrassment. He chuckles.)

G: You're right. *Matalena* was scary with an eye pointing West and the other East-Southeast. I never knew when she was talking to me or the guy on the other side of the road. So embarrassing. *Cose 'e pazz.*

A: I have a question for you. Why didn't you speak Neapolitan when you were young while you are doing it today?

G: I don't know, maybe because I wanted to leave this shitty place. You, on the other hand, have always spoken it and left before me.

(Antonio stretches out an arm and places his hand on Giorgio's shoulder)

A: I have never hated Naples and my being Neapolitan. I was not too fond of this place because it did not give many opportunities to those like me. Just as you hate a woman you love who doesn't love you back.

G: Let's say you convinced yourself you didn't hate Naples. Furthermore, you ran away when you were 18 because you loved her.

A: You don't get it. I ran away because it was too tight for me. I had no prospects, and going to the North was the opportunity of a lifetime for me. Then I realised that the problem was not Naples but all of Italy.

G: That bad? Even then, I remember you predicted that Italy would become Neapolitan?

A: When I arrived in Verona, I had other problems. They disliked me because I was Neapolitan. In the end, I spent three years between Venetia and Lombardy. Still, I escaped abroad where screw it, for the first time, I was Italian and not a peasant from the South, a *Terrone*, or a Neapolitan.

(Giorgio nods, showing that he understands and shares Antonio's thoughts)

G: Yes, I also had problems in Milan, I must say. It was not a walk in the park; however, the fact that I spoke Italian helped me.

A: Hold on… Didn't I speak Italian? I don't understand. Bro, I was already writing articles for the local party newspapers and was a radio speaker. Maybe you forgot that.

G: You're right. I was saying that without thinking.

(Antonio interrupts)

A: Who wrote the poems for your wife? You? I remember when you called me in London at midnight because you had a fight with your girlfriend and to make it up you told her that you had written a poem for her. Two hours and I had to produce something for a person who, you know very well, could never stand me.

G: True, I remember that night. How clingy we got. She accused me of not being romantic enough.

A: By the way. Now that you're separated, can you tell me what the fuck I did to your wife?

G: Never mind; she was weird.

A: She was, but so were you. Ultimately, we broke a friendship for her because I don't think I ever did anything to you. Listen, shall we have a game at Scopa?

(Giorgio seems to want to divert the discussion and responds excitedly to Antonio's proposal)

G: Fuck! But yes, go ahead. Oreste, will you give us some cards, paper, and a pen? Thanks.

A: Let's go.

(The two walk toward the inner room where no one is and remain as dreary as in their memories. They both look at the room, but neither of them comments)

G: I can't even remember the last time I played cards.

(They take their seats at the small table where they can keep an eye on the bar counter with Oreste serving customers)

A: Shuffle well! You used to do tricks. Do you remember?

G: What a laugh! With Franco and Rino! They didn't understand how come they always had shitty cards.

(Giorgio laughs, and Antonio follows his friend).

A: So why did your wife dislike me? You didn't tell her about the poems, did you?

(Giorgio sighs as if he has to perform a massive effort)

G: No, not at all. That's an old story.

A: Tell me about it. I am dying to hear it.

G: So let me think where to start.

(Giorgio thinks hard)

G: When we first met, I was always talking about you. She was jealous. So that's why she never wanted to meet you.

A: And that's all? But do you think I'm dumb? Don't let it be known, or I will no longer sell a book. By the way, have you ever read a book of mine?

G: Not really.

A: And why is that?

G: Because it bothered me that you had become famous, and even the idea of contacting you seemed to be a way to brush shoulders with someone famous and not because I wanted to contact you.

(Giorgio reacts to his own words. As if he said something he should not have said, expecting a reaction from Antonio)

(Antonio grimaces in disbelief)

A: So you thought about contacting me? Why didn't you do it when your mother died. I contacted you and even gave your brother the number. Don't give me the bullshit you gave me earlier on because I know that you contacted Antonio Borrelli, Franco, Rino, and God knows how many more.

(Giorgio seems to be surprised)

G: But... why... are you in contact with them?

A: Yes, it's about ten years now. Then, when they brought up WhatsApp, we created a group. Do you want to distribute the cards?

G: Yes, wait. Shall we play three games at 21?

A: Sure, yes.

(Antonio signals to shuffle the cards well).

A: So why couldn't your wife stand me, but, please, the truth this time?

(Giorgio lets out a sigh as if he needed to find courage for what he was about to say)

G: My father. It was his fault.

A: Meaning?

G: When you began to write professionally, but even before that, and your articles began to appear in major newspapers as well, followed later by programs on the national and international radios, my father began to discredit me in the eyes of my then-girlfriend.

A: If my father had admired you, I would have been happy. Unfortunately, you know that was never the case.

(Antonio says this with a note of piqued satisfaction).

G: My father saw you as the perfect son. Writer, intellectual, respectful, with clear political ideas. I also started voting for the Communist Party because of that. Because my father was a socialist. My fiancée could not stand my father humiliating me in front of her.

A: I don't understand. Your father's making trouble, and I'm the one who pays the consequences?

G: You know what women are like...

A: I think so, but I also know what men are like, and I don't think you'd been a man. Am I wrong?

G: I wanted to live quietly. So, to make her happy, I tried to disengage from you as much as possible. You did the same thing when you engaged with that schoolmate's sister. Do you remember that?

A: I remember the little girlfriend, but not that I had distanced myself from you. In fact, there were so many fights because on Saturdays I was going out with you and not with her. Do you remember?

(Giorgio looks surprised)

G: No, wait. She couldn't go out all the time on Saturdays.

A: That's what I used to tell you. The truth is that I told her clearly that I didn't want to break the friendship with you, so some Saturdays, we had to skip our dates. At first, it went well. Then it bothered her, but I continued seeing you on many Saturdays.

G: I didn't know that.

A: Did I have to write it at the end of the books I was writing? Ah no, then I wasn't writing books. Whatever... You understand what I mean.

G: Yes, I understand.

A: Fuck! You got distracted!

G: What a lucky sod!

A: You left the 4 on the table, knowing there were three still out while there were no more nines.

G: There were two 4s out already, clubs and spades.

(The discussion comes alive but in a joking way).

A: You're dreaming! Remember where we are, and if the other two 4s come out before the game ends, I'll give you two extra points.

G: No, you're right. It's the conversation that is getting a little heavy.

A: Relax! It's been so many years anyway; it's not worth getting angry or having scruples or regrets. The past is past.

(Giorgio seems to acquiesce)

A: So you, for love, have broken our friendship. And isn't that such a condemnable thing? Ultimately, you had to choose between living quietly and being yourself. In fact, surely there was no choice because you are yourself when you live quietly. But, at least, did you manage to live quietly?

G: Let's say for twenty years we were okay.

A: For twenty years, you never talked about me? I'm joking. Continue

(Giorgio smiles and continues)

G: Then the problems started. It was hard to adjust because she had a major career opportunity and two children already. My job allowed a lot of free time, but there were shifts, and I couldn't change them as I wanted. She would get pissed off.

A: You could call the defence secretary, get him to talk to the army general, and change your shifts.

(Antonio stands at guard mockingly).

G: At ease. Exactly. He didn't understand that I didn't have the same contractual power ordinary employees have. So she wanted me to change jobs.

A: To do what? Excuse me, but someone with your experience, what else can he do?

G: Retire and wonder what the fuck I've done all my life at work.

A: But it was early for retirement?

G: Indeed. And that began to cause issues. We began to fight even in front of the children. We got a babysitter who cost me more than my salary, and she wasn't happy either. Her job required a lot of commitment, even during weekends and especially a lot of money for clothes, shoes, and makeup. In short, her and my salary were insufficient for the fixed expenses.

A: Wasn't she aware of this?

G: She said I had to take care of it because I was the man of the house.

(Giorgio mimics the sarcastic facial expression of what should be his wife)

A: You are the man on demand. When you had to stop talking to me, you had to be a woman.

G: Yeah. I wish that was the only thing I had to go through. Every month, she met a new man, colleague, and client; they were all real men with balls. I, on the other hand, the usual asshole. Let's leave it at that. You, on the other hand, why did you break up with the foreigner?

(Antonio snorts, clearly stating that he almost doesn't care to talk about it.)

A: These were completely different dynamics from yours, but in the end, the outcome was the same. As you can see, and you'll remember, I said in an article that there are many ways to scan a sheep, but the result is that it always dies.

(Giorgio laughs and slams his hand on the table, blowing up the cards).

G: Fuck! Yes, I remember! How pissed off the communist, Sen. Shephard, was!

A: The communist? Why weren't you?

G: I used to pretend. I was never a communist. I told you why I did it.

(Antonio touches his forehead with the palm of his hand).

A: How many votes have we lost because of your father? If Craxi had known it!

G: I became an army man, the opposite of being a communist.

A: Whatever, if you were in Russia, you would have been consistent with the choice.

(Pause for silence while they play cards).

G: So, how did it go for you?

A: Wait, let's check these points. Do we do it the simple way or the scientific one?

G: Let's simplify it, or we'll spend the night here.

A: Okay, then me, 3 points

G: No, that is not right; one point is even.

A: OK, then make up your mind, simple or scientific?

G: Let's make it simple, you're right!

A: Keep the scores, and now I'll shuffle the cards.

(Antonio passes the notepad with the pen to Giorgio).

A: Unlike you, I never got along well with my wife. Let's say we were friends. Then, nothing more. Love was never there.

G: And why did you get married?

A: Do you think people who marry for love then stay together forever? Along with sex, it is the first thing that disappears. All it takes is one more burp, one more fart, or how you drink broth or if you don't shave, the female starts hating you.

G: True.

A: So we were very good friends. We used to have fun. She wanted to travel the world like me. I mean, there was no sign that there would be a blizzard.

G: But it happened...

(Antonio nods his head and has a facial expression suggesting that it was worse than a storm)

A: Yes,it did happen. When my wife got pregnant, she became another woman. Unrecognisable. Then, when my son was born, it was even worse. She began complaining about everything and especially wanted to settle in one place and own a house.

G: I don't see anything strange. They are all like that. When children are born, it's like they've taken out a life insurance.

(Antonio nods)

A: I accommodated her and bought a house in North London. She wanted it in Wimbledon, where we had lived before we moved to Switzerland. But I had no money to buy it there. In the end, she settled. The contentment was short-lived, though.

G: Of course...

A: More and more demands and more and more expenses. Then, my wife complained that I wasn't helping around the house. Just so you understand, I was still working in Switzerland and came home every weekend for three days. Then, the money wasn't enough. I mean, it was a constant complaint.

G: And what did you do?

A: I went back to England, but then she complained that the money was less than before and that I was always late at night. In short, a pain in the ass that was resolved with an unspoken separation. I was minding my own business, and she was minding hers. Things began to improve in the sense that we were no longer fighting; however, we were growing more and more apart, and if it hadn't been for the baby, we might have even said goodbye.

G: In all this time, have you never talked about divorce?

A: Twelve years passed to get to the separation.

G: Why did you then separate if everything was fine?

A: Why do you think? Because she had found someone else and fell in love. I knew it would happen to me or her sooner or later. So we divorced.

G: Did you suffer from it?

A: Economically, and that's all. How about you?

(*Giorgio hints at an expression of pain*).

G: I have. Recently, I've been starting to see positive aspects, too, but it was initially very dark. I used to see her everywhere and miss her every aspect of my life.

A: Has she met someone else?

G: Yes, in my opinion, since before the separation.

A: I guess. It seems that some people suffer from the Tarzan syndrome.

G: What is that about? Never heard of it.

A: It doesn't exist; I made it up in one of my books. It seems that some people don't feel complete unless accompanied by someone. So they tend to cling to a liana and then precisely leave the previous one, like Tarzan.

(Antonio mimics Tarzan going from one liana to another)

G: I have to write it down. I like it. I can use it, right?

A: Only if you get the book.

G: Point for me!

A: How bloody lucky!

G: Did you see that? Now you got distracted! You, keep talking...

(They both laugh)

A: Distracted? Look at the cards! I have only 5's in my hand. Who the fuck shuffled these cards?

G: You!

(They keep laughing)

A: Ah. True. Hey boy, can I have an Aperol spritz?

G: At this time?

A: Oh yes, do you want one?

G: A Crodino.

(The young waiter comes running in and hints at noting down the order)

A: A Crodino and an Aperol Spritz, then. Thank you.

(The boy doesn't write anything down and leaves the room).

G: Me, one point then. You, four.

A: So, 3 points plus 1, that's 4, and you 2 plus 4 makes 6. You're ahead.

G: Did you have any doubts?

(Giorgio smiles; Antonio follows with a sarcastic laugh)

A: Yeah, yeah, keep teasing. It's only the second round; shuffle well!

(They don't speak for a few minutes. They seem to be running out of topics)

G: Remember when we spent whole afternoons trying to invent magic tricks?

A: Surely do! Your grandmother, the poor woman, used to be the audience. "Look who we have in the audience. There she is, that lady in the second row. Madam, please join us on the stage."

(Antonio stands up and impersonates a curvy old lady who can barely walk. Giorgio cracks up laughing)

G: And my grandmother saying, "What the fuck are you talking about? I don't understand."

(They both let out exaggerated laughter as if reliving the exact moment when the situation occurred)

A: Please, ma'am, help us with this game of magic.

G: Then she would come to the so-called stage, and every time we pulled out a card, she would say that was the one she had picked. She would see the ace of clubs and then say it was the 3 of gold... What a laugh!

(They continue to laugh almost hysterically. Oreste peeps in to see if they are okay. Antonio nods reassuringly. Oreste laughs and goes back to the counter)

G: We were supposed to take Grandma onboard and perform a comedy show around Italy. So much for magic. If I'm not mistaken, we never managed to get one right. I'm talking about the tricks. Or am I remembering wrong?

A: You remember wrong. We made five hundred thousand lira disappear in one night.

(Giorgio seems to be surprised).

G: I don't remember.

A: Think it through. The party we organised, the MacPi!

(Giorgio beats his thigh with one hand. Mimicking an expression of pain)

G: Jeez, what a bloodshed that was!

A: The whole of Naples had to come, but in the end, we had to ask our parents for half a million to pay for the premises.

G: Your father was pissed off!

A: Yes, instead, your father was jumping for joy. He had me do the maths to see how many years it would have taken for you to pay back those two hundred and fifty at 10 per cent by paying ten thousand lire a month!

G: And how long did it take, do you remember?

A: Wait, I shall do the maths now!

(Antonio pretends to do calculations, looking at the ceiling)

G: Come on!

(Antonio laughs)

A: You are dumb! Anyway, it was almost three years.

(Giorgio seems to be surprised).

G: Are you joking?

A: No, why?

G: You didn't change a bit! That's so you. When I say something to my children jokingly, and they take it seriously, I say, "You look like the children of Antonio's old soul."

A: Thank you for the old soul. You had really buried me. Did I have a good funeral, at least?

G: That's a figure of speech

A: Or a Freudian slip.

(Giorgio chuckles)

A: Eh, you are joking, but the situation is getting serious.

G: What is serious about it?

A: That you allowed me to make two improbable points.

G: Shit, but you distract me.

A: It was all premeditated. I'm going to annihilate you today. Metaphorically speaking, of course.

(Giorgio starts checking points)

G: So, one point for me and 5 for you. Overall, me 7 and you 10.

(The busboy arrives with the drinks).

A: So, where are we? Thanks for the drink, boy. But next time, we'd appreciate it if you could bring them before lunch.

(The boy nods, puts the glasses on the table and leaves)

G: Anto', you're in Napule, not in Zurich? Or wherever you are these days.

A: I'm in London. Are you still in Milan, or have you changed areas?

G: No, since I separated, I have lived in Monza.

A: And the children? Back and forth between the two houses?

G: The kids, no longer children, stay where and when they want. The mother's partner seems to be nice. I've only seen him in photographs. So they come and go between my house and their mother's.

A: And don't you have someone now?

(Giorgio shrugs)

G: I don't feel like it. I'm better off alone, honestly.

(Antonio seems almost surprised by the answer)

A: I don't know. The English say you can't live with but without them either.

G: We should have a wife-on-demand. Like the TV apps.

A: Wife on demand, the new App...

(Antonio laughs with a sarcastic and incredulous expression)

G: Not a bad idea, though...

A: Are you starting with another entrepreneurial idea? How many have you had?

G: A shitload.

(Giorgio spreads his arms wide)

A: How many have you put into practice?

G: None.

A: Here you go, this might be the first one! Go for it. Who distributes the cards?

G: You, here you go.

A: Remember when we wanted to go to work in the nudist village in Spain?

G: It wasn't a nudist place? If I'm not mistaken, it was a swingers' village in Ibiza.

A: Yes, but it was for naturists.

G: Are you sure? I didn't remember.

A: We sent the letter with pictures of us. How old were we? 15, 16?

G: More or less, we were certainly not of age.

A: Caros segnores...

G: No, come on! We wrote it right. We used the Italian-Spanish dictionary from the library. Then let's say we didn't write it so well when we received the owner or manager's answer.

A: Dear Antonio and Giorgio, first grow a little bit in height, then you can spend a vacation together with us as a... gay couple! We have many bisexual guests who would find you attractive, but before then, practice a lot.

(They both laugh)

G: What a laugh!

A: That was so embarrassing! Who knows what the fuck we wrote to make them think we were a gay couple.

G: Did we write? You wrote! I just went to the post office. You did the whole thing yourself. Like always!

A: Meaning? Like always, what?

G: Never mind.

(Antonio becomes serious)

A: No, no, tell me. After so many years, it's interesting to discover that maybe your wife was right.

G: Anto', you were always the brain in our friendship. You were the one who planned everything, who, in the end, also decided for me because you made sure that whatever was organised, there would always be pussy and music. That was enough for me. On the other hand, you just needed cigarettes and being left alone, in peace, to read and write. Sometimes I wonder: how the fuck were we friends?

A: You still don't get it? Because we weren't busting each other's balls. I wish I could find a woman like that! Do you want to see that the Spaniard had seen right through us, and we missed an opportunity?

G: You know the laughs around here. They would have been enjoying playing the lottery with the elements in that story. They'd still be playing the last numbers after 40 years!

(They both laugh)

A: Then there was the job in Montesilvano.

G: Don't remind me of that. What a summer that was!

A: I never understood what really happened that summer. I don't think you ever told me the whole story.

G: That was more than forty years ago. But I remember those six months as if it were today, I must say. What happened was that I went to work at that hotel, Il Silvano, for the summer. You were already in Verona or Milan; I don't remember anymore. I met this Swedish bird, and since I was studying Swedish and English in college, I have found an opportunity to practice. Then you know... my insane passion for women... Two days in bed, screwing non-stop.

A: Of course. The rabbit.

G: Every day, several times a day for two weeks. This one's dad was an Arab. I don't know from where, but he wasn't Swedish-minded, so we did everything secretly.

A: Which didn't stop you.

G: Hell, not! Then they went away to Gothenburg, and we stayed in touch. I would write postcards, and we would phone every now and then, and, at Christmas, I was meant to go to see her, either in Gothenburg or in Denmark, where she had enrolled in university. At least that's what she said.

A: Why wasn't that the case?

G: One morning when I was home, it was October, I think, the police came with a summons. I didn't know what the fuck they wanted, and they told me that I had been accused of raping a 16-year-old girl.

(Antonio follows with pre-occupied attention)

G: I didn't know what they were talking about, and they gave me this letter where they explained that this girl, pregnant, 16 years old, had stated after months that she had been raped by a certain Giorgio Tommasi in Montesilvano. Repeatedly, even.

A: Fucking bad story. So you were also a dad. Or maybe you still are? I didn't know all the details. I only knew that you had been accused of sexual harassment, but then you had managed to prove your innocence, and it was all settled.

(Giorgio laughs bitterly)

G: But what innocence? Today, there would have been evidences. At the time, there was no way to prove your innocence. She would never write to me. She used to call me, so there was nothing written. It was my word against hers; as you know, women are always believed. Then I had a reputation as a whoremonger, and it didn't help because, in the meantime, other clients from the hotel, with whom I had fucked, popped up, and there was a massive disaster.

A: And your father...

G: My father didn't believe me. Only my mother and Tonino, my sister's boyfriend, believed me. Then, neither did my brothers. In short, it was a mess I can't describe.

A: And how did that get resolved?

G: It was resolved because the bitch, during a hearing in court, made it clear that the father, to save the honour of the family and not to send her to his home country in Arabia to live, had asked her to know the name of the child's father and accuse me of raping her.

A: Typical of certain cultures. You read about it every day in English newspapers.

G: She who had informed herself well in her own country and who wanted neither to have me arrested, let alone go to *Islamistan,* took advice from an association that protects Arab women in these conditions and decided to speak out.

A: But you had slept with a minor anyway.

G: Yes, for that, there was a light sentence, but since it was consensual and other various bits and bobs, I got off with a smack on the ass and a little time with social services.

A: What about the baby? Was it yours?

(Giorgio jerks up from his chair as if offended).

G: No, the child was not only not mine; he was black. So the slut had done it with someone else.

A: Wow, what a story!

(The two return to look at the cards on the table)

G: So, me 7 and you 10. Who deals?

A: I don't know, it's up to you. It's all the same, anyway.

G: No, no, come on you. It would help if you didn't complain later when I have demolished you.

(Antonio looks around and towards the counter)

A: Boy! Where the hell is he? Boy, another Aperol Spritz. Do you want a Crodino, Giorgio?

G: No, go ahead. I'll have the same as you.

(Antonio scrambles to get someone's attention at the bar).

A: Two Aperol Spritz then. But put in a little Spritz and more prosecco and Aperol this time!

G: I will go to my sister's house crawling.

A: But what do you care? You only live once.

(They laugh)

G: Fuck!

(Antonio jerks in fright).

A: What the fuck! But how do you score a point like that? Didn't you shuffle the cards like you did as a kid? With a catch, you made four points. That's crazy stuff!

G: I have to admit. What a lucky sod I am!!!

(They laugh in delight)

A: Ah, thank goodness for that!

(Giorgio suddenly becomes serious)

G: Excuse me for asking you a very personal question. I can, right?

A: You ask it first, then see if I can answer it.

G: No, I am sure that you can answer. It's a question of whether you want to answer.

A: Go ahead. I'll try.

G: When the mess happened in Zurich, people here asked many questions.

(Antonio gets sad)

A: Here? And what were you doing here?

G: No, my brothers and parents were telling me.

A: Okay, go on.

G: So, are you going to answer me?

A: Yes, go on; I shall answer to your question. I already know where you're going with this.

G: Then don't make me ask the question. Is it a yes or a no?

A: Yes.

(Giorgio has an almost pained expression. As if he had hoped for a different answer)

G: Ah, then it was true. I was hoping it was not.

A: Why? Is that a problem for you?

G: Yes and no.

A: Explain. I don't understand.

G: I understood that something had happened, but I didn't dare to ask you about it, much less talk about it.

A: Neither did I, as you may have guessed since it came up thirty years later.

G: And it happened to me, too.

(Antonio remains astonished. He doesn't say anything for a few seconds)

A: Ah, I didn't know that. I'm sorry. Still the same asshole?

G: Yes. Always him.

A: And how did you get over it?

G: By writing. Yes, I'm not as good as you; however, I used to write too. I used to jot down thoughts, how I felt, etc. Finally, after years, I reread everything and saw that it didn't affect me anymore. I burned everything, and that was gone.

A: And why didn't you come forward when I made the appeal?

G: Because I was ashamed. Almost as if it was my fault.

A: But you already knew it wasn't your fault. Right? If you had spoken out, it would have brought out other people who were victims of that shit, and Ciro would not have committed suicide unnecessarily. Instead, the bastard died at home and of old age, that big shit!

G: Anto', you've realised I'm not a big man.

(Antonio bristles)

A: No, I understood that you only think about your own shit. And you don't hesitate to betray anyone and any idea so that your matters go as you want them to go. Congratulations!

G: No, it's not like that. I knew it wasn't my fault. But I didn't want to end in everyone's mouth like they did with you. You don't know how much they said about you.

A: And I don't give a damn either. I do know that I was the only one to confirm what Ciro had written in his suicide letter, while the other four all kept quiet. The poor man. He died in Zurich, away from everyone.

G: I suck.

A: Confirmed. You suck. When I saw the dead body, I never thought it was Ciro. Just because he looked like his father, I could tell it was him. I made them take me to where they found him. Do you remember the pond in San Giorgio? That's it. It was like that, including dead animal carcasses and dumped washing machines and sofas.

(Giorgio tries to get up).

G: Maybe I'd better go. I feel like this conversation, this meeting today is making me feel like shit.

A: No, it's not the conversation. It's the fact that you're finally talking about things that should have been said years ago. But most of all, you're hearing the other side of the story. I've suffered a lot from this distance you've taken toward me. I never understood the real reason.

G: I'd better go!

A: Of course, your wife hated me; I knew it, but why and why you, who have been my friend for 16 years, had not seen fit to talk to me. Even to tell me you didn't want to talk to me anymore.

G: I know. You're right.

(Antonio gets up from the chair, swaying as he looks up).

A: To think that you are in the army. Let's hope there will never be a war; otherwise, you'll lose it if they're like you.

(Antonio points his finger at Giorgio)

G: Okay, look, Anto, I'll go then.

(Antonio pushes him down on the chair while Giorgio tries to get up)

A: Where are you going? Let's continue the game, and as I said before, let's talk openly without lies and hypocrisy. Giorgio dear, maybe this is the last time we meet. Let's pretend that we are confessing. Then we'll say goodbye, and if you want to, or rather certainly, you'll erase everything, at best, I'll write a book about it, and I'll also make some money.

G: What a piece of shit!

(Awkward silence)

A: Ahhhh... So, you scored 5, and me nothing. You 12, me 10. I'll shuffle now, though.

(*Giorgio gets up and goes to the counter*).

G: Marittiello! Where are the Aperols? I need two just for myself.

(*He returns to the table*).

A: Wait. I'll order two more so we don't have to ask again.

(*Antonio stands up but almost loses his balance as if seized by a sudden illness*)

G: Watch out. You were falling.

A: It's the excitement!

(*Antonio jokes. Trying to minimise what happened*).

G: It must be the Aperols!

A: You don't know how many drinks I down daily, and I don't even notice. Wait.

(*Antonio leaves the small room. He goes to the bar and comes back a little later*)

A: Here you go. I brought them; otherwise, Marittiello would bring them to us for dinner. Cheers!

G: Cheers to you!

(*They drink without speaking to each other. Then, Antonio resumes the conversation*)

A: If I may return to the conversation from earlier. How old were you when Don Ciro took advantage of you?

G: Maybe 12 years old. You?

A: I was 11. Until I was 14 years old.

G: And how did you survive all these years?

(Antonio doesn't seem to want to talk about it).

A: Weren't you supposed to go to your sister's for lunch? Do you have at least 10 hours for the whole story?

G: No. I'm sorry.

A: So, I'll try to be brief. It's one hour we talk, and in two hours you have lunch. Do you always eat at 1 pm?

G: More or less. We kept that tradition. Remember, right, how pissed off my mother used to get when we were late for lunch?

(Laughs, Antonio)

A: Of course! It was a sacred thing! So, where do I start... Sorry, but even now, it's not easy to talk about it.

(Giorgio reaches out and touches Antonio's hand that was resting on the glass)

G: Don't worry about it. If you don't want to talk about it, it's okay.

A: No, no. I want to talk about it. So, do you remember when we used to go to see those Italian B-movies? Once I went to the cinema with Salvatore Crispo and Bernardo Melito. They left after a while because the movie was one of those you were waiting to see a pair of tits; instead, they never showed them.

G: Of course! You used to call them the scam movies.

A: I stayed because I had paid 500 lire and I wasn't leaving early. During the intermission, I went to ask a guy sitting in front of me for a cigarette who had been smoking the whole time, and it was him.

G: The twat.

A: He told me to keep him company. I sat beside him, and we chatted for the whole movie. Maybe, actually, he definitely hadn't recognised me. He got up to go to the bathroom and asked if I wanted to go too. Needing to go, I went.

G: Oh my God.

A: While he was pissing, I noticed that he was looking at my cock. And he showed me his. I felt a little ashamed and was about to walk away, but he grabbed me by the shoulder and took my hand and made me touch it. I tried to pull away, but he told me it was normal and that they played this little game that he liked, even with his son.

G: What a piece of shit!

A: Yes. Knowing the son, I thought it was a normal thing. Dad had never told me anything about sex, and, as you know, we knew little at that age.

G: Yeah. We only knew about sex from the pornographic newspaper clippings that those older than us left around.

A: He told me to go inside a toilet because this was supposed to be a secret. We went inside, and he wanted to put it in my mouth.

(Giorgio has tears in his eyes and looks at Antonio as if it was the first time he had heard such a thing)

G: But I said no. I don't know why I was afraid or instinct made me react. He didn't really budge. He told me to sit on the toilet, which I did, and he stood in front of me with his legs open and started masturbating. Then he told me to wait a little while and come out.

G: What a shame. What a coward...

A: Ah, I forgot. The bastard left me a thousand lira and told me not to tell anyone about this.

G: And you?

A: I waited for him to leave and left as soon as I heard he had left. I didn't go back to the cinema; I went home. It was already evening. When I got home, I felt strange. I don't know what it was; however, I felt like talking to Gino, although I don't know why.

G: And did you go there?

A: No, the next day, I met Gino at school, but I didn't know what the fuck to say to him. It's not like I could ask him if his father was getting his thing touched?

G: Maybe he would have confirmed it.

A: I don't know. I know we became better friends with him because of his father. I started doing my homework with him, and we also went to the fun fair on Sundays.

G: I remember that time.

A: One afternoon, while we were studying, his father came in. When he saw me, he whitened. He didn't expect me to know his son. He pretended not to know me, but then when I left, he stopped me on the ground floor, took me to the basement and told me that if I talked to anyone, he would hurt me and he would also hurt my parents. I got the confirmation then that it was not something appropriate.

G: He did something similar with me, too. Continue.

A: A few days passed, and I saw him everywhere. One night, he followed me home, took me to the basement and made me touch him and abused me.

(Giorgio raises his hands, then puts them over his ears).

G: Anto, that's enough. Let's skip the details. I feel sick just thinking about it.

A: Yes. Let's skip to how I managed to get it out of my mind. For years I didn't know whether I was a fag or not. When I masturbated, I would always think of him. I would start with a beautiful woman, but I would come with him. By now, I was really only attracted to him. Not men, just him. He had already stopped molesting me. Maybe I had gotten too big for him and certainly too hairy. Then, we know he had moved on to our poor friend, who committed suicide.

(Giorgio lowers his eyes in shame).

G: With me, it lasted a little. Only a couple of times. But it was enough to screw me up. I never masturbated in my life because of him. It reminded me of him and, therefore, a dirty thing.

A: Ah, that's it. Now it's explained. I remember you didn't do that. For me, with Marisa, my first girlfriend, it was a tragedy. Two years together, never a fuck because, for me, it was a dirty thing. It had to be years before my first relationship with a woman. It was with that woman older than me that you certainly remember. I was 18, and that same year, I was going to leave for Verona.

G: I remember too well. I was jealous. I didn't lack women, yet when you were with Marisa and Marianna, the married lady, I envied you. That fucking radio had made you famous. Yes, I was jealous of you but also envious.

A: Shit, you even remembered the lady's name. Bravo. She was a wonderful woman. 36 years old, beautiful, very rich and, above all, in love with me. I wasn't in love with her; I realised it later, but I liked living the good life. I felt like a man, male, after years of uncertainties.

G: But it was short-lived.

A: Yeah, it ended badly, very badly indeed. The husband found out everything and crippled her with blows. Then I learned that they broke up and she died years ago of cancer; she was very old.

G: Antonio. I have to confess something to you. You're going to hate me, but you told me we should tell each other all the truths and clear our conscience.

(Antonio is intrigued)

A: Tell me.

G: We went to the phone booth one afternoon because you had to call Marianna. You forgot the card with her phone number.

A: I remember. In fact, I couldn't call her for days, and she came over to the radio to give me the number again.

(Giorgio lowers his eyes)

G: I took the card.

(Antonio freezes. Surprised, a few seconds of silence between the two, then continues)

A: How? Why?

G: I told you. I was jealous. But that wasn't all.

(Giorgio pauses while Antonio waits for him to count).

G: I called that number, and a man answered. A month later, I got the number. And I told him that his wife was cheating on him, but I didn't tell him with whom.... I'm sorry!

A: Don't...

(Antonio gets up and walks in a circle. He looks very disturbed by the news. He clenches his fists. He starts cursing indistinctly in English)

G: Anto, say something. Please don't leave me like this. I'm sorry. I was young! I was jealous. I was always jealous of you and envious of the way you were. Wasn't it just my father who thought you were a hero? If I went to the army, it was because my father paid someone; otherwise, they wouldn't have wanted me there either. Forgive me, please...

(Antonio leans on a chair away from the table, looking in the opposite direction. With tears in his eyes)

A: I don't feel well. I need to get some air. I had imagined a conversation like this but never expected such infamy. This is even worse than the refusal to see me in Milan. Sorry, but now I'm the one who wants to leave.

(He heads for the exit. Giorgio reaches out to him, also in tears)

G: Forgive me. Forgive me. No, no, let's finish this game.

(Antonio goes into a frenzy. Customers from the bar enter the small room to see what's going on. Antonio is furious)

A: And you think I, I give a shit about the game after what you told me? You're bloody joking? How many years did I wonder how the husband could have known? For years, I distrusted the radio people and my classmates. But you. I never doubted you. Never could I have thought such a thing. You might as well not have told me. It would have been better.

(Giorgio sends everyone away and returns to the table).

G: It must have been the Aperol to speak.

A: Then you are the proof of the saying that the barber makes you handsome, the wine makes you a bully, and the female makes you a sucker. Remembering your vanity, you proved all three elements of the saying right. You are a real twat.

(Giorgio nods, still with tears in his eyes).

G: I was. True; now I've changed a lot.

A: I bet; you are sixty years old. Did you still want to be a child?

G: I don't know what to say. Maybe we'd better go.

(Antonio returns to the table, very angry).

A: Surely, it would be better, but I want to see what else comes up. 12-10, you're ahead. Let's continue this game. We change it a little bit, a twist. With each point, you can ask the other person a question, and they have to answer it honestly. Wine makes you brave; let's take advantage of it because I've had a few questions to ask you for the last 30 or 40 years. All right? Here you go! The cards!

G: I don't know. I don't feel comfortable.

(Antonio is furious. Angry as never before)

A: Oh yeah? Now you don't feel comfortable? Hand out the cards.

(Giorgio is almost afraid of Antonio and hesitates to answer. He would like to leave but knows he can't)

G: Okay. But no scenes because they came in from the bar into the room when you raised your voice.

A: And since when has this place been a library?

(Giorgio tries to calm his friend by indulging him).

G: Okay. Go. Let's do as you say. I guess you don't want to tell me any more about how you managed to make peace with your past as an abused child. Do you?

A: Giorgio, you don't make peace with the past. You put it aside and accept everything, knowing you were not at fault. That's what I did. It took 40 years to do it, but then I did it. I spent more on psychologists than cigarettes, but then I made it in the end. Is that enough for you, or do you want the details?

G: Fuck! That is a point for me.

A: Bravo. Ask me the question.

G: No, I don't want to ask you any questions. I don't deserve any answers; honestly, I don't think I have any questions for you. I know you were always a real friend to me. No, give it a miss this time.

(Antonio is furious)

A: Ask me a fucking question! Now! Or I'll get really pissed off!

G: OK, OK, OK, calm down. Let me think.

A: Look. The pasta will get cold if you don't hurry.

G: So Here. Have you ever fucked a man?

A: And what kind of question is that?

G: I don't know. It just came to me like that.

(Antonio shakes his head from side to side).

A: You haven't really changed. You still think about the same thing today at sixty years of age. But I'll answer you without a problem. No, I have never fucked men. Happy with that?

(Giorgio gasps)

G: Sorry for the embarrassment. I didn't expect it. You know, the rumours...

A: And why are you embarrassed? Don't tell me it was you who let everyone know that Mario and Filippo were gay? What rumours?

G: No, no, it wasn't me. When we saw them, it was me, you and Gino. I always suspected you, Honestly.

A: Ah, thank you! So, if it wasn't you, it was Gino. Now we know.

G: It's your turn. Go.

(Turns to the young barboy who had never left the small room given the interesting discussion)

G: Marittiello, bring a bottle of prosecco now.

A: A bottle? I wonder how many more things you have to tell me. If you're looking for courage, pretend you drank a cask of wine and tell me everything. Let's stop playing games, too.

G: No, no. Please, let's continue. But let's get this point thing out of the way.

A: Point!

G: Fuck.

A: Too late. I'll ask the question now.

G: Go ahead. I'll be honest.

A: A question I've wanted to ask you for a long time, and you partially told me while making excuses for your shittiness. How come you got into the military, someone like you who was alien to discipline? What was the trigger?

(Giorgio feels uplifted by the question).

G: Easy question. Good thing. After the Montesilvano thing, dad told me that I had completely screwed up. He didn't trust me. I needed discipline to become a man. So he paid Marshal Crispino to let me join the army.

A: This we all knew. Crispino not only took the bribes but also bragged about it. Continue.

G: Father paid about fifteen million. I didn't know anything. I didn't want to leave my studies when I got the call, but he told me he would throw me out of the house if I didn't accept.

A: Maybe you would have become a man since the military didn't do much good.

G: We fought for a week, and then I had to give in. Especially when I learned that he had paid that respectable amount of money months and months before. So I left for Turin and started this shitty career. Then I began to get used to it because, in all honesty, I wasn't doing and don't do shit from morning to night, and I had time to go fooling around here and there until I met my wife.

A: How did you feel when you met her and were doing a job you didn't like?

G: Then the problems started between her and you.

A: Me? Me? What problems? I saw your wife twice. A week before my wedding and on the day I married. That's almost forty years.

G: No, I mean the problem that led me to break away from you. One weekend, I returned to Naples and told my father I wanted to leave the army. My father got really pissed off in front of my girlfriend and gave me shit, taking you as an example. That's when Maria Elisa said you and I should never see each other again.

A: You stayed in the army, though.

G: Yes, the money spent was too much, and my father, as he did with the five hundred thousand lire of the party, did with the fifteen million he had paid. But then, Antonio did not do the calculations, and to this day, I feel that I still have not paid them back.

A: Maybe it was convenient for you.

(*Giorgio is nervous*)

A: But tell me, have you been faithful to your wife all these years?

G: Doesn't it seem you've got an extra point? Am I wrong?

A: No, you're not wrong. At least you have time to think about the next answer.

(The bar apprentice arrives with Prosecco).

G: Thank you, Marittiello. Would you also bring us two clean glasses?

A: Then you have four points, and I have two. You got 16 points, and I got 12.

G: But do you consider yourself bisexual?

(Antonio looks at him between curious and angry).

A: Excuse me?

G: No, about the question about sex and males. Do you consider yourself bisexual?

A: Actually, I don't consider myself anything. I never had sex with men. Why are you keeping asking?

G: Yeah, whatever, but would you do it?

(Antonio shakes his head but catches his breath and answers calmly)

A: I have been with many women never a man. I tend to fall in love and with men this would never be possible. I liked the courtship, the flirting.

G: I only fell in love with my wife...

A: With men, it was something in my head, a fantasy.

G: I get it. Did you know there was gossip about you and your school friend, Ariosto?

(Antonio looks at Giorgio with curiosity)

A: I never knew that. Ah, these are the rumours you were talking about. Sometimes I wonder where the fuck I was when you guys were gossiping!

G: No, these are stories that came up after you left. Some even said your father sent you away to break up a relationship with that Ariosto.

(Antonio laughs out loud, explaining himself at his table).

A: Ariosto, Carmine was more of a womaniser than you! Queer, my arse. I ran away from here because I wanted to escape the miserable chit-chat, the dirty past, the constant badmouthing. I ran away because I wanted to prove that I wasn't running away but was running toward something. And I proved that enough. Didn't I?

(Giorgio looks almost mortified).

G: I would definitely say so. Aside from a few people who made some fortune, you are the neighbourhood's pride. After all, you're really self-made. And you've changed more trades than all of us put together.

A: Well, let's say that here, between soldiers, sailors, police officers, and thieves, there is little variety in the trades. You all live off someone's back.

G: Thank you for the compliment.

A: You said it yourself that you haven't done shit all day for 40 years.

G: How do you, on the other hand, make a living? Who puts the food on your table?

A: Readers, viewers, newspapers, TV, radio in half of Europe. I don't see the comparison between a military man who has never fought a war and someone like me who instead makes a living from his work and author's books, articles, and film treatments. Do you see that?

(Giorgio raises his hands as if surrendering).

G: Fucking hell, how touchy you are. It was just an innocent question.

A: After all these revelations, I doubt anything is innocent in anything you say. And ever since we met, you've been filling me with bullshit. We started with condolences and ended with the latest news you gave me about your responsibility for the breakup of Marianna and her husband's marriage.

G: Well. You said you wanted the truth. I'm giving it to you. You hand the cards, go!

A: Okay. I'd say let's stop at twenty-one and then forget about it. I wouldn't want you to skip lunch.

G: You don't worry about me. Just distribute the cards.

A: You're five points short. Let's see if we can figure it out.

G: Ah, I wanted to ask you a question. Who is Carmela?

A: Carmela, what do I know. Who is she? Should I know her?

G: Carmela, the character in your book, *Vite a Meta'*.

A: Ah, sorry, I thought you referred to a real person.

G: Then she's not a real person?

A: No. A character from a book. As simple as that.

G: And why do I feel like I know her?

A: Didn't you say you had never read one of my books?

G: In fact, I haven't read any. I saw the show on TV when they made a movie out of it.

A: Did you like it? At least?

G: I only watched half of it. Then I got bored and went to bed. My wife watched it until the end. The next day, I saw she put a 5-star review on a site.

A: Wow! Mrs. Maria Elisa has forgiven me! But you were already separated?

G: No, we were still together, but it was ending. She knew that; I didn't.

A: Carmela. Carmela is an assortment of characters I have come across in my life. She also has a lot of me. And maybe of you, too.

G: I knew it! Of me, she has the fact that she's a slut. Of you, on the other hand?

A: Of me, she has everything else...

G: Easy!

A: But why? Who did you think she was?

G: To me, she reminded me of the lady on the sixth floor who used to be a prostitute and then got married to Mr. Piscopo.

A: That one was fifty years old when I was ten. Who knew that woman?

G: Whatever, there was a lot of talk about her.

A: Giorgio, it occurs to me that although we lived in the same building, you and I lived two completely different lives. You seem to know everyone's businesses! As the English say, you can take the guts out of the pig but not the pig out of the guts. It seems you never left this shithole.

(Giorgio seems to take offence, but he holds back).

G: Let's say you were very distant from everyone. You didn't give a shit. You were only thinking about you, politics, study, ambitions. You were too focused on your ego to think about others and look around.

A: You didn't consider what was around me too disgusting? That I didn't care about the gossip and all the crap that was being said about everyone? Even about your sister's scandal with your married neighbour?

G: Shit, I thought you didn't give a shit.

A: In fact, I didn't give a fuck. I was hearing and letting things get over me. Did you understand that I didn't care about all this talking?

G: Maybe you did. Maybe instead, you thought you were a little superior to look around yourself.

A: Maybe you're right. Hearing you talking, though, I think I would have been right. Or wouldn't I?

G: I used to think you were an intellectual. Now, I think you were already a snob when you were young.

(Antonio pretends to laugh noisily and raises his face to the sky)

A: I'm still a snob, right?

G: Well, yes. Don't you recognise that you feel superior to the rest of us?

A: No. Different, yes. Superior no.

G: Points of view. My wife used to say that you would die alone because you tended to alienate and distance yourself from others and your roots.

A: Die? What the fuck does that mean?

G: According to her, you wouldn't last long because of your dissolute life, and you would always be alone and unhappy.

(Antonio continues his nervous laughter).

A: Well, she seemed to know me well, the one I've only seen twice, and she only told me once, "How do you go around the world. I get lost even in Naples." A very smart woman if she understood everything about me after two sentences exchanged.

G: She knew a lot more about you than you think.

A: Well, she seemed to be obsessed with me more than anything else.

G: No, Maria Elisa is an incredibly good connoisseur of the human psyche. Remember that she is an amateur psychologist, but a good one.

A: She looks more like a psychopath to me. So, if your wife is a good person and mentally stable, were you foraging her dislike for me? I'm beginning to believe. In fact, I'm not beginning to believe it; I'm convinced I was right when I thought the real shit was you and not that woman. There was an uncle of mine who once told my mother that he hated us. He was talking about us children.

G: And why did he hate you?

A: He grossed us out because my grandmother did nothing but talk to him about us and praise us. Here, you must have done the same thing. You and your father. But at least your father with admiration, while you with envy and resentment because, in your words, I was like you wanted to be. And you were not.

G: Fuck!

(Antonio shakes his head)

A: Go, you're only a few points away!

(Giorgio suddenly stands up with his index finger in the air as if asking permission to speak)

G: Question.

A: Shoot.

G: Don't you miss a normal life?

A: And what would be a normal life? In England, 66% of couples get divorced. So I'm normal. In England, you change jobs between 5 and 15 times in your working life. I am normal. In England, you retire at 67 years old. I'm very normal.

G: I meant the life you could have had in Naples or Italy.

A: And what do I know what life would have been? I miss the family. I miss the food. I miss the dialect in the streets. Going to the stadium to watch Napoli's matches. But how do I know what a normal life is? Do you lead a normal life?

G: I would say definitely not.

A: See, if you were in England, at least for the divorce, you would be normal. Otherwise, no. One job all your life and soon to be retired.

G: Can I ask you a personal question?

A: Yeah, because we've been discussing the weather so far.

G: So to speak.

A: Go ahead.

G: Have you always been faithful to your wives?

A: Not to the first wife, as I told you. We lived separate lives. I also fell in love a few times but wouldn't lose my freedom. Did you?

G: Only once. But it's an insignificant thing.

A: Look, you don't have to justify yourself. In fact, congratulations. Knowing you, I would have expected affairs aplenty.

G: No, I was always in love with my wife, and it was the alcohol that made me do something I regret to this day.

A: We'd better stop drinking then! I wouldn't want to tempt you.

(They both laugh)

G: There is no danger. I've never liked blokes.

(Silence between the two).

G: My wife said the book of the kidnapped child was a masterpiece. But the fact that you had written it put everything into question.

A: Sorry, Giorgio, but do you always speak your wife's mind? I didn't understand if you were happily separated or lying to yourself. You seem to have no opinion about anything. Am I wrong?

G: No, I meant to say that according to my wife....

A: Again?

G: No, my wife...

(Antonio interrupts stymied)

A: That's enough! Please tell me what you think, not your wife. Who gives a shit about that bitch!

G: You're right. I realise that I have no real opinion about you. Everything I think about you, it's not my point of view. What a shitty man I am.

A: Whatever; maybe after today you'll have an opinion.

G: I wanted to read the little girl's book; you know? I read the plot and liked it. Then I let it go.

A: And where did you read the plot?

G: My wife had the book. She brought it home one evening with another, The Ghosts of the Past. It was then that I started smelling a rat?

A: Because of my book? Your wife had my book? But are you sure she hated me?

G: No. She held the book in Italian; she held it very dearly. She was strangely happy that night. Then, in hindsight, I understood everything.

A: Meaning?

G: That night, she fucked her lover, who then is now her partner, Andrea.

A: And what do you know about that?

(*Giorgio continues as if hypnotised*)

G: I saw her strangely happy after weeks of being pissed off. Then she left the book in the hall cabinet and ran straight to the bathroom. She usually asked about the boys while taking off raincoats. I know her well, and that evening was all different.

A: I imagine what a monotonous life you would have if you knew each other so well.

G: Even when she came out of the bathroom, she behaved differently than usual. Also, she had sent me a message telling me she would be late for the office, while I saw she was at the Galleria near the Duomo.

A: Shit, are you even following her?

G: No, we have always had Google tracking. An old technological discovery that we have never repudiated. I mean. She wasn't in the office that night. Then, the tracking took her to Corso Vercelli, where she stayed for a few hours. When I asked her where she had been, she said she had been in the office until 7 o'clock and then gone to dinner at a restaurant on Corso Vercelli with a colleague.

A: So she had skipped the visit to the Duomo.

G: Yes. I also checked Google for restaurants nearby, and there was only one hotel. The Splendor.

A: I know it. I go there sometimes when I'm in Milan. It's a pleasant hotel, but it's not one of those hourly hotels. The publisher pays me for it, and it's 300/500 Euros a night. He must be wealthy, this lover she had found.

(Giorgio shrugs)

G: Well, I don't know. He works at an interior design company. He's an architect.

A: So what did you find out? You said she had left my book in the lobby.

G: Yes, I opened it, and there was a dedication that sounded strange to me.

A: What did it say?

G: More or less, it said, "Dearest, you could have been the muse that…

(Anthony interrupts)

A:" ... I didn't know... to... look for...with affection..."

(Giorgio is surprised and jumps out of his chair)

G: And how do you know?

(Antonio is embarrassed and can't hide it).

A: Let me see a picture of your wife. Do you have any?

G: I have one from a couple of years ago, maybe three.

A: Let me see it.

(Giorgio peeks into the phone and, finding one with the family, zooms in on her and hands the phone to Antonio)

G: Here she is.

(Antonio whitens. And breathless and speechless, and hands the phone back to Giorgio)

A: The game is over. Bye Giorgio, sorry but I have to go. It was a mistake, this meeting. I'll pay the bill.

(Giorgio gets up from his chair suddenly by extending his arm and holding Antonio still in his seat)

G: You are not going anywhere. Now you explain everything to me. Stand still; let's not make a scene.

(Antonio would like to get up and points his finger toward the bathroom door)

G: No, you're not going anywhere. Just pretend I scored a point, and tell me everything you know.

A: Pour some prosecco; this one won't be easy to tell.

(Giorgio ignores the request. Antonio tries to take the bottle, but Giorgio blocks him)

G: You! Now! Talk! And don't sweeten the pill. What the fuck do you know?

(Antonio looks at the cards on the table and puts down his own, taking a very long breath)

A: Okay. I saw your wife twice, as you know. Decades ago. I didn't even remember what she looked like. Three years ago, I was in Milan for the book presentation that would later be followed by the readers' signing. I mean, something you do a lot and may have even seen in movies on TV.

G: Cut to the chase!

A: At the end, when the queue of readers was over, a woman approached, a beautiful woman who, unlike the others, told me that she did not want any book signing but only to have coffee because she wanted to talk about a book of mine as she had doubts about the integrity of some facts. Honestly, the Neapolitan accent, the beautiful presence and the perfume induced me to say yes without even thinking about it. Besides, I was to fly to Paris the next morning, and this woman intrigued me.

G: I guess I know who she was.

A: Yes, it was the woman in the picture. Your wife. But I didn't know until now. I'm sorry.

G: Are you sorry? You slept with my wife, and you tell me you're sorry? Then you were not sorry? And why did you make the dedication on the book to her like Antonio and not like Pascal?

(Giorgio is furious and gives Antonio no time to answer, who stands there, mute)

G: You knew it! You, piece of shit! It was your revenge. Your revenge!

A: What the fuck are you talking about? Asshole! Who knew your wife? If I knew it was her, I would have spat on her face, that's all. Do you realise what a bitch she is? She came to the presentation on purpose to spite you! But do you get it or not? Asshole! Asshole! Asshole!

(Oreste, Marittiello, and other bar guests enter preoccupied but are watching and listening. Antonio turns to them)

A: This asshole; he has a slutty wife and takes it out on his friends! Fuck off!

(Giorgio gets up suddenly, throwing the table, the bottle, the glasses and the cards in the air, and grabs Antonio by the neck. None of the bystanders interfere)

G: I'm going to kill you! Because of you, my life is shit! Do you understand that?

A: Your life is shit because you are shit. You always have been, ever since you were a kid! You are a man with no balls! You are not even worth a thimbleful of shit! Your father understood that early! It's a good thing he's dumbed down now, so he doesn't have to see what a big piece of shit you've become.

(The two continue to hold each other but do not fight. The bar guests are escorted out by Oreste, who tells the two that they must leave the bar)

G: I can't believe it. You slept with my wife.

A: I slept with a no-good, who was then also your wife!

G: Did you at least enjoy it?

A: Yes, very much, and if I had known she was your wife, I would have liked it even more!

G: Fucking twat! You can show off all you want, but you're not worth shit! Bastard! Arrogant bastard!

A: You're sick, Giorgio. Let a doctor see you!

(*Giorgio begins to cry, sobbing and holding on to Antonio, who won't let go of him*)

G: What did I do wrong? Why did she cheat on me with you? Why? You who are intelligent, tell me why she did it.

(*Antonio caresses Giorgio and tries to calm him down. Oreste insists for them to leave*)

A: Oreste, we cannot leave in this condition. Give us ten minutes, then we'll take off. We've given enough clues to play some numbers anyway; go to the lotto counter; you have enough numbers for the next twenty contests.

(*Oreste walks away. Antonio makes Giorgio sit where he was sitting earlier. Giorgio does not stop talking incomprehensibly*)

G: Why? Why?

A: I know why. But calm down, and then I'll explain since you don't get it.

(*He leaves him at the table and starts picking things up from the floor*)

A: Just so you wouldn't lose at the card game, you got yourself into a fit....

(*Giorgio laughs between sobs*).

G: Always joking. Does anything ever stop you?

A: No. Not even death. You know that, don't you?

G: Sure. I remember at the funeral of Concetta, my brother-in-law's sister. We never laughed so much. After an hour, it looked like it was a baptism...

A: That was such a shitshow. I remember.

G: Maybe, but it was one of my most enlightening moments. I realised who you were. You were not even 17 years old, and it was clear what you were made of. And it bothered me. I admired and loathed you for your confidence and your charisma. I told myself then that you were going to go a long way, and I could only have sex with those few ugly girls to feel superior in at least something.

A: Giorgio. Don't say those things. You're not that bad.

G: You told me so much this morning that if I don't kill myself, it's because I have two children.

A: No, dear brother, to kill yourself, you need balls. And you don't have any.

G: Shall we start again?

A: No. In fact, it's time to stop. We've cleared everything up, I think. We know who we are, what we did, and most importantly, what a shitty friendship we had.

G: We're not done. Explain why that bitch slept with you.

(Antonio breathes a sigh of relief as if to give himself a boost of patience)

A: The short version is because she hates you.

G: What about the long one?

A: It takes a day.

(Oreste arrives with glasses of water and looks at Antonio, making a sign that they can stay longer)

A: Thank you, Oreste. Excuse us. I'll pay for your trouble and damages.

(*Oreste walks out, making a sign with his hand as to say not to worry*)

G: So? The medium version? The long one, I guess, is too long.

A: I guess the problems between you and Maria Elisa were old. From your stories, it seems that you took each other for granted. Always condescending, you knew the steps you were taking, what time you were shitting. In short, an old couple. But you were not old.

G: True.

A: I don't know if you ever tried to talk about problems or if you knew you had problems. Clearly, your wife was suffering, and you didn't even realise it. Your wife didn't feel she was being treated the way she wanted.

Moreover, you, to make her happy about everything, demasculinised yourself. A gutless one, indeed.

G: But she should have been happy...

A: Eh, no. When you're not married, you're nice. After married, you're dumb. Before marriage, you're good. After marriage, you're dumb. You should know these things.

G: But she never told me anything.

A: People want to be understood. She chose to make a mockery of you by screwing the person she hated the most. She didn't even tell me her real name. She said her name was Nina. But she told me not to put her name in the dedication. And expressly asked me to sign it with the initials of my real name.

G: Why did you call her a muse?

A: It was a joke. When we had dinner, Elisa asked me some serious questions about some of the events in the story; as a joke, I told her that if I had her as a muse, my book would be twice as long. She laughed like crazy. Thinking about it now, I should have seen that it was all fiction.

G: Why do you say that?

A: First, because the next day, I found her comments taken from some reviews on Amazon. So they were not hers. And then because something didn't convince me about what she was saying. She sounded like a, how should I say, someone well-travelled. But on the Internet, not in real life. But honestly, though, I liked her and did what I did. I fucked her, and she was another fuck on my list. Sorry for the vulgarity.

G: No, no. You did the right thing. You're right.

A: Believe me, I didn't know it was her. I wouldn't have ignored her, but I certainly would have had a conversation similar to the one we're having now.

G: I don't understand why she didn't tell me if she wanted to hurt me.

A: Well, she did it for her own satisfaction. She knows she did it. And unfortunately, so do I. Sorry, you know it now. Are you going to tell her?

G: Not a chance. Too much satisfaction.

A: Bravo.

(Both in silence, looking at each other).

G: Still, it was a tough morning. For both of us.

A: Yes, it was needed, though.

G: Shall we finish the game?

A: Get over it!

(Laughter)

G: I think Oreste thinks we're crazy.

A: If it were only that. Now they all know our shit.

G: Who gives a fuck.

(Antonio puts his head in his hands.)

A: I have a confession to make.

G: Eh, no, eh! Enough.

A: No, listen. It's important. More than anything, we've said so far.

G: And what could it be? Tell me. Please don't keep me waiting. By now, you can even tell me that you are the Messiah. Nothing surprises me anymore.

A: I wish it were that simple.

G: So what?

(Antonio thinks. He's about to start talking. Then he stops)

A: I don't know where to start. Please don't interrupt.

(Giorgio nods)

A: I arrived in Naples the day before yesterday. I had informed Gennaro and Franco that I would arrive that evening. They told me you were here. I came especially to see you. So, this morning was not a coincidence. I was waiting for you. I was on the balcony, and when I saw you, I came down.

G: I don't understand why?

(Antonio signals to him not to speak)

A: I didn't want to leave without seeing you.

G: I don't understand. Sorry. What do you mean?

A: I had to understand what had happened. Why did you completely erase me from your life? That was something I never accepted. And now it was time to understand.

G: Okay. I think we have talked and understood each other now. No?

A: Yes. I can leave now. I'm going away, sad. Because I know that ours was not a real friendship. But most of all, we are no longer what we were.

G: Anto, I don't understand anything.

A: Don't worry. Let me give you a hug. Be sure to do good things and take care of the children. Bye Giorgio.

(Antonio turns and walks away without looking back)

G: Antonio!

(Antonio ignores him)

G: Anto'! Fuck! Get back here!

A: What do you want? You haven't cared about me for over twenty years, and now you don't want me to leave?

G: No, I just wanted to tell you that I don't agree with you about our friendship.

A: Meaning?

G: In my opinion, it was a true friendship that then spoiled because of jealousy, envy, arrogance, ambition and especially because of our individual passions.

A: Explain what I would have erred in that; so far, I have never seemed to make any mistakes in what I thought was friendship with a capital F.

G: I have told you before. You say that I, to pursue my objectives, am willing to do anything. Whereas you? You left Naples overnight. It was July 7. I remember it like it is now. The day before, after you graduated from high school, you knocked on my door at eight o'clock at night to tell me you were leaving for Verona the next morning.

A: Do you remember what I said?

G: I could go with you, and we would have many adventures.

A: What about you? What did you answer? Do you remember?

G: No, I was too sorry and shocked.

A: Then I'll remind you. You said you didn't feel like going against your father's will and needed the money because you had to go to Sweden. It was your life's dream, and even friendship is not worth a dream.

G: I said that more or less. I remember. And you said goodbye and left.

A: Yes, and I called you every day, even when you were in Stockholm. Even though I had two thousand lire a day to eat. Sometimes I didn't even eat to phone you.

(Giorgio lowers his eyes)

G: I didn't know that. I thought you were doing well, economically speaking. See, the pride. Couldn't you have told me? Or were you too proud?

A: I didn't want my only friend to worry about me. But these are finesses that you will never understand. Pride doesn't have a damn thing to do with it.

G: Antonio, shall we start again? I'm willing to change and return to what I was for your friendship.

A: Giorgio. Neither you nor I are what we were.

G: But then, what the fuck did you want to see me for? To humiliate me?

A: No, I had to determine whether ours was a friendship. And now I have the answer, and I'm appeased with my conscience.

(He gets close again. Antonio hugs Giorgio. He then pulls away)

A: Bye. Have a good life.

G: Same to you.

Three months later.

Gennaro: Hi, Giorgio. I'm sorry to tell you this via WhatsApp. I tried to call you all evening, but you didn't pick up. Antonio Russo is no longer with us. He died this morning in London. His wife told us. He died peacefully at home, surrounded by his children and wives. He had been sick for a long time, at least six months, with lung cancer, but the condition worsened last week. When you can, call. A kiss.

ACT TWO

(Giorgio is sitting in his armchair. He has a telephone in front of him on the coffee table. He also has a bottle of whiskey. He looks at the phone, hesitant. Then he pulls it up and presses a number. The saved number of someone he frequently contacts)

(Maria Elisa is slicing vegetables while smoking)

Maria Elisa: Hello Giorgio.

(Pause of silence)

M: Hello, Giorgio. Are you there?

Giorgio: Yes, yes. Hi Elisa. Yes, this is Giorgio. I'm here.

M: I know it's you. Tell me, I'm in a hurry; I must prepare tomorrow's dinner.

G: And are you going to prepare it tonight?

M: Why does that sound strange to you?

G: No, to say. It was just curiosity. Do you have guests?

M: Yes, friends of Andrea's. Tell me. Do you want to talk to the boys?

(Silence)

M: Giorgio. Can you hear me?

G: Yes, yes, sorry. I'm here.

M: So, tell me. Do you need anything? Are you okay?

G: I'm fine. Thank you.

(Silence)

G: Actually, I'm not well.

M: What's going on? Do you need a doctor?

G: No, it's not that kind of sickness. It's...

(Starts to cry)

M: Giorgio! What's the matter? What's going on? Speak.

(Continues crying)

G: He's dead! He's dead!

M: Oh, my God. I'm sorry. Just so sorry. Giorgio, he was 93 years old. I'm sorry. If you can, come by tomorrow, and we'll talk in person. I would also come to Monza, but I just can't.

G: No, Elisa, my father is fine. Antonio Russo died.

(Silence on both sides).

G: Gennaro wrote to tell me. He called me all day, but I didn't look at the phone because I was redecorating the bedroom.... Antonio... my friend...

M: I'm sorry. When did he die?

G: This morning. Let me forward the message to you.

M: Okay.

(Maria Elisa looks at the message)

M: I read it. I'm sorry. Really.

G: I had seen him in Naples three months ago. We didn't part well. Now I understand why he wanted to see me.

(He starts crying again in sobs).

M: Don't do like that. He had a good life. He did what he wanted and, most importantly, achieved things that none of us can even dream of.

G: He was smart. He was the best of all of us kids.

M: Do you plan to go to the funeral?

G: I don't know. I haven't really thought about it. Should I? What do you say?

M: I don't know. It's up to you. Do you have a passport?

G: Yes. But I don't know if I should.

M: He would have liked that for sure.

G: Not after the things he said to me last time.

M: I don't know what he said to you, but maybe it was anger....

G: He said that ours was never a real friendship.

M: Definitely a moment of anger. Did you have a fight?

G: It was surreal. All surreal. I don't fancy talking about *'o fatto.*

M: *Ué,* are you speaking in Neapolitan now?

G: Strange. He had told me the same thing.

M: Come on, you're slowly rediscovering your origins. By returning to Naples so often, you're becoming a *Terrone* again.

G: I've always been a *Terrone.*

M: I'm glad for you. I am Italian.

(Pause for silence)

G: I've decided. I'll ask Gennaro for his wife's number and the funeral's details. Wait till I ask him.

(Writes a message and returns to phone).

G: I have asked him.

(Pause)

M: Giorgio, are you there?

G: I was thinking. I wonder if it would please him if he were alive.

M: He isn't. So you have to do what pleases you, not Antonio.

G: Okay, I'll book the plane tonight. And the hotel.

M: Giorgio, I'm sorry. I'm sorry, but I have to go now.

G: He's not there?

M: Andrea. No, he's not here. He's coming home late. You? Why don't you see some friends? I sense that you're not well.

G: I'm staying with Jack tonight.

M: And who is he?

(Giorgio turns a glass over in his hands, filled with whiskey)

G: Daniels, Jack Daniels. Whiskey. The only friend who can give me some relief tonight.

M: And since when have you been drinking?

G: Since I realised how many things I've done wrong.

M: Mind you, I could empty the liquor cabinet if I had thought about my mistakes. Giorgio, the important thing is to look forward and learn from the mistakes made.

G: What about me? Was I a mistake for you?

(Maria Elisa puts down the knife she was cutting vegetables with and sits down at the table)

M: I wondered about that for many years. Then, I stopped because I didn't particularly appreciate where the train of thoughts was taking me. An acquaintance once told me that happiness is being able not to think. Or maybe I read that somewhere.

G: So what? Mistake or accident?

M: Giorgio, I don't think this is the right time to discuss such things. Now, put down that glass and see if you can get some distraction.

G: I'm not. I'm saying this calmly. Tell me if I've been a fucking mistake for you.

M: No, you have not been a mistake. All right? Now, however, I have to go.

G: Instead, you were the biggest mistake of my life.

M: Good. I'll go now that I'm busy. Good night.

(Maria Elisa throws down the phone)

G: I realise that I still love you, though.

(Giorgio looks at the phone and notices that Maria Elisa has hung up)

G: Look at this bitch!

(He redials, this time in full, without using the saved number)

M: Giorgio, go to sleep.

G: If I wasn't a mistake. What was I?

M: But do we have to talk about this right now? Giorgio, you are not in the right state to talk about things you never wanted to talk about. But what the fuck happened in Naples when you saw Antonio again?

G: What happened is that Antonio showed me who I am, who you are, who I could be, and, most importantly, who I will never be.

M: And that would be?

G: Antonio. I will never be an Antonio. I never have been.

M: What is that supposed to mean?

(Maria Elisa sits back down, pours herself a glass of white wine and lights a cigarette)

M: Go on, I got some popcorn; let's hear what he said. Let's see what revelations your youthful idol made during that famous meeting in Naples. In whiskey veritas.

(Giorgio laughs)

G: Ah, dear Elisa. If you only knew how many things he told me. And if you only knew how many I told him.

M: If you want to talk, I'm here. Otherwise, I'll go back to the stove.

G: The kids? Aren't they at home?

M: No, the big one is with the little girlfriend, and the other is at a friend's house in the building. A family from the south moved into Mrs. Zeda's apartment. The daughter didn't want to sell it, so she's renting it. They are from Puglia. Good people. Actually, no, they are from Lucania

G: I would exclude the Lucani from the Kingdom of the Two Sicilies!

M: And what is this news? You always got along well with the Lucani

G: No, no. I was thinking about what Antonio had told me. He was pissed off with the Lucani

M: There you go! The champion of the weak was also racist!

G: Hell no, we were joking. It was only blokes' talks.

(Giorgio's cell phone vibrates)

G: Wait, I have a message. Then. "Hello, Giorgio. The funeral is the day after tomorrow. This is the address of the church. St Johns the Baptist, London, etc., etc." OK. So, the day after tomorrow I'll be in London. I'll finally visit it.

M: That's good. It will certainly be good for you. Maybe stay a few more days.

G: How about I take the kids with me?

M: Giorgio. They have school. It is already hard to let them attend regularly; let's not put strange ideas in their little brains.

G: You're right. I'll go alone. Maybe someone else from the circle of friends will go.

M: That wouldn't be bad. If I know Gennaro well, he will already be there to be photographed by the paparazzi. He's always on Instagram.

G: And how do you know that?

M: I follow him. And he follows me.

G: I didn't even know you were on Instagram. That's new to me.

M: It's new that you asked me. I've been on Instagram for years. Actually, many posts are starting to pop up for Pascal de Napoli. His wife put the news on his official page. There are a shitload of comments already from all over the world.

G: He was famous, Pascal. But nobody knows Antonio.

M: I wonder if Antonio hadn't been dead for a long time, leaving room for this Pascal guy.

G: So you were following him? Pascal, I mean.

M: Yes. All along. But not on socials because he had no account.

G: For someone you didn't like, not bad.

M: I used to follow Pascal, not Antonio. He was a good writer. Politically, I never understood him. But he used to write about politics on various sites, newspapers, or even in his books. But others used him as they wanted. He would never reply. Even the Neo-Bourbonic put the page in mourning.

G: But he was not one of them. He told me that clearly.

M: Those would also use the Savoia's to get some visibility.

G: He didn't believe in Italy as a nation, though.

M: Giorgio, I see you're feeling better. I'll go back to doing my thing.

G: No, please. No. I wonder how it is that we are talking. And for the first time in years.

M: Oh yes. We needed Antonio's death for us to talk. The one who didn't talk to you for years, and we don't even know why. Or did he explain it to you? I must say it's very honourable of you to have forgiven him. Bravo, this is the Giorgio I like.

(Silence)

M: Are you there?

G: Yes, yes. I'm here.

M: I was saying that it's a credit to you.

(Giorgio interrupts)

G: I heard that. I've heard. Thank you.

M: Ah, okay. You were silent.

G: So I changed over time?

M: Well, we wouldn't have divorced or separated if we were what we used to be. We both changed, but we lost each other.

G: I stayed the same. You have changed with your career ambitions.

M: I mean, me, a Uni graduate, raising two kids, was I supposed to stay home and be a wife waiting for her soldier boy? You are crazy.

G: The soldier boy has always respected you, appreciated you, made you live the good life over the years, and you still spit on it.

M: Did you ever ask me what I wanted all these years?

G: Why did I have to ask you? Couldn't you talk?

M: In fact, I talked, and it all went to shit.

G: You talked when it had already gone to shit.

M: Whatever, the phone and whiskey are not the ingredients for such a discussion. Maybe we'll talk in person when you have time.

G: I always have time. You're the one who's busy all the time.

M: Unfortunately, I'm not a soldier.

(Silence)

G: Anyway, I'm looking at the flights. I'm leaving tomorrow night from Linate. I asked Gennaro if he was going. He's already in London.

M: I told you. He put his profile in mourning on Instagram. I didn't know they were so close, the two of them.

G: Antonio told me he had gotten close with some of our friends. It must have been the need to come to terms with the past.

M: With you, on the other hand? Nothing. Next, you'll tell me why he didn't talk to you for 30 years, the fucking intellectual.

(Giorgio becomes infuriated)

G: Shut up! If it weren't for you, we would have remained friends. You're the one who made our friendship break up! And that didn't help to keep you happy either. Only your friends, your colleagues, your family. None of those on my side were ever good enough for you. No, they were not up to your social status! The countess of this dick!

(Maria Elisa responds in kind).

M: You are completely out of your fucking mind! But who the fuck ever told you to break a friendship? Who broke away from your family? When did you ever propose to see any of your friends? Giorgio, you don't speak. You infer. Then you blame others.

G: Because I know you too well.

M: No, you don't know me at all! You don't ask. You assume I would inevitably say no, and then you don't ask. So, regardless, it's my fault. Grow up, you little brat! Grow up! You're about to retire, and you've never been an adult. That's why Antonio wanted nothing more to do with you. Forget the bullshit. Go blame him, the poor guy! Look at you tonight.

(Giorgio is silent)

M: Anyway, I don't want to continue this conversation. Use the pension money for a psychologist rather than the kids' collection of toy aeroplanes. Giorgio. Grow up! You lost your friends and a wife; don't lose the family too. Good night!

(Giorgio hangs up without saying anything)

(Maria Elisa lights yet another cigarette and pours another glass of wine. She goes to the vegetable cutting board. She bangs her fists on the counter and sweeps everything away up in the air before slumping down to cry)

(Maria Elisa picks up her cell phone and makes a call. She's very upset)

M: Hi. We need to talk. We'll hear the two truths now that I'm tipsy, too. And don't hang up on me.

G: Actually, I didn't hang up.

M: You don't blame me for the breakup with Antonio, do you? He was the one who never contacted you. Not us, certainly not me. I must have seen this Antonio no more than a couple of times. It was always you who didn't let me meet him. I still don't understand why.

G: Antonio is not to blame. I broke off the friendship because I thought you disliked him.

M: Me? And why should I have disliked him? He was the only one in your group of friends who wasn't a loser. He was the only one who worked his ass off to get where he got. Giorgio! You are sick!

G: No, it bothered you when my father talked about him and said I was nothing compared to him.

M: It bothered me, true, but it was your father, not Antonio, who pissed me off. What fault was there with him?

G: So you liked him, even.

M: Who ever met him? We had been engaged for a couple of years when you introduced him to me with his future wife. And he was nice. He was cultured. He was kind. I mean, what the fuck was there not to like about him?

G: You said no when he asked us to be witnesses.

M: I said no because my mother was not well, and we had to go abroad to be their witnesses.

G: But you told Antonio that you could not even orientate yourself in Naples, let alone abroad.

M: Giorgio, my mother was not well. You knew that; the rest of the world didn't. The last thing my mother wanted was for the world to know about her depression and suicidal delusions. Fuck! What an asshole you are!

G: Maybe you're right.

(Maria Elisa interrupts abruptly).

M: Now, you tell me what the fuck you said to each other last time. You're making me think that, in the end, I was to blame for everything. Let's hear it out! What did he say? Why didn't he contact you again?

G: He reminded me I didn't want to see him once he came to Milan.

M: Is that true?

(Giorgio is hesitant, embarrassed)

G: Actually, yes.

M: But I didn't know anything about it. I would have been pleased. When was this happening?

G: In the year 2000. He was in Milan for work; his wife and son were there too. He called me in the morning, and I told him we had guests in the evening and were preparing dinner, so I didn't even have time to meet them for a coffee!

(Maria Elisa lets out a suffocated cry).

M: But you are such a twat! Thank fuck he thought I was the bitch! Why didn't you tell me?

G: I thought that...

(Maria Elisa interrupts)

M: You always think, you're always thinking, and then you don't think about the consequences when you do things. Thank God that he wanted to see you before he died. I would have written about my little twat of a friend on social media in his place!

G: I was wrong in trying to avoid trouble with you. I thought you would have been pissed off.

M: Wait, wait, wait. So, if I understand correctly, Antonio didn't break the friendship with you, but you were the one who cut him out of your life because you thought I disliked him? That explains a lot, but really a lot.

G: Well, he didn't even contact me anymore though. And, if you remember, he didn't even come to our wedding.

M: Giorgio, but he was right not to contact you. And our wedding was before two thousand. He was in Australia on business and sent us a massive gift, saying he would spend that money on clothes, travel, and gifts. He was a gentleman because you were already not talking to him by then. If I remember correctly, the last time you spoke to him as a real friend, you told me you had gone to Montesilvano for the summer. We got married years later. And he kept contacting you.

G: Well, yes. True.

M: So what did you tell him? Why didn't you contact him? Why did you break the friendship?

(Giorgio doesn't know what to say. Then, quickly).

G: I told him that you couldn't stand him...

M: What a little man you are! I couldn't stand him? But did you ever ask me? You stopped talking about him all of a sudden. I thought you had a fight, and I didn't want to ask you anything because I know what you're like when you have your things.

G: When I was talking about him, you were making a crooked face, grimacing!

M: Of course! You were always talking bad about him. You were always critical. What did you expect? I form an opinion about people based on what I see. I can only go by what they tell me if I don't see. What the fuck did you expect me to say that he was nice when you kept saying that he was arrogant and belittling you, that he had stopped contacting you... Let me figure out what's the fucking truth since the poor guy died thinking I hated him.

G: Nothing. And everything. But so you didn't hate him?

M: Is this you or Jack talking? How the fuck can I hate someone I don't know. Do you think that if I hated him, I would have bought his books? Would I have followed him around on the Internet? Giorgio, really, get a shrink to move in with you. You are sick. Very sick.

G: What have I done! I destroyed the lives of two people!

M: No, Giorgio, you destroyed your life and our marriage. I have a happy life, and Antonio had a great life. The one left holding the match is you. Antonio wanted to see you before he died to understand what happened. Unfortunately, he left with the wrong explanation.

G: No, I don't think so.

M: What are you trying to say?

(Giorgio gets up from the couch and fills another glass of Jack Daniels).

G: Wait. Let me remember the exact words.

M: How much are you drinking?

G: It helps me to talk freely. Even with Antonio, I opened up when I was tipsy.

M: Suit yourself. I want to know the truth. Behind this story is your whole personality. Understanding what you said to each other also helps me understand who I lived with all those years and who the father of my children is.

G: We talked about the past, about the doings of the sexual assault and the suicide of our friend. I mean.

M: I mean... What do you mean? Okay, since you don't understand, then I'll ask you the questions, and you'll answer me.

G: Okay, maybe that's better.

M: Other than me being the monster who destroys other people's friendships, what else did you tell him? For example, the bitching that you've reported to me over the last 40 years.

G: I told him he was a coward. I told him he was arrogant. Things like that.

M: And why would he be a coward?

G: He ran away from Naples. He put the abuse story aside. He didn't even report them, only to jump out when Ciro committed suicide to get some free publicity.

M: I didn't know Antonio well enough, but he was anything but a coward. In my opinion, Naples was a tight fit for him. And about the abuse story, tell me, but if it had happened to you, would you have gone to the police? Or even to your parents?

G: No. I didn't go to the police, much less to my parents.

(Maria Elisa is surprised. She drops her cigarette and tries to extinguish it so as not to burn herself)

M: Fuck, I got a hole in my new pants. Wait. Let me understand. You were abused? Why didn't you ever tell me?

G: Because, at the time, I didn't feel manly enough. I always wanted to have sex with women when I was young to prove that I was a male.

M: And you never thought you could tell me such a thing?

G: No. I never had the courage. I buried it completely, and when Antonio spoke from Zurich, it rekindled something. Still, I didn't dare to come forward.

M: Not even after the death of that poor boy? I would be ashamed of myself if I were you. Other than Antonio being arrogant and getting publicity. The problem is you. You're the one who has no sense of shame or empathy. You are the one at the centre of the world! Good thing you didn't pursue a military career. Do you know what disasters you would have made out of your cowardice?

G: You don't understand. You didn't go through that. Those were awful years. Years of almost weekly violence.

M: But did you tell Antonio?

G: Yes, I told him, and he gave me some shit because I didn't talk.

M: I mean, he didn't say anything about it. You know, something like "I'm sorry. How are you? How did you feel?"

G: Very marginally. He pushed the button of the sense of guilt that I should have for what happened.

M: Okay. Of course, save the people who only have acquaintances if this was a real friendship. Tell me, how were you able to deal with these ghosts growing up?

G: I initially convinced myself, then realised it wasn't my fault. He stopped when he found another victim, younger than me. I was sick for years, though. The only way to escape it was to screw left and right.

M: Fight fire with fire. Good philosophy.

G: No, it wasn't. I just wanted to prove I was male.

M: Prove it to whom? To yourself. To the women you said you loved and then left them after a fuck, you were proving anything but that you were male.

G: True.

M: Did you ever think those women were losing trust in males? But what did Antonio tell you when you told him about your sexual adventures?

G: He was not interested in sex. It is because of what had happened to him. I don't know. But he enjoyed listening to my tales when I talked to him about them.

M: I wonder why I have a completely different idea about Antonio. But I want to believe you.

G: I swear it's so.

M: Wait till I get a book; I want to read you a sentence.

(Maria Elisa leaves for a few minutes, then lights another cigarette. She gets up again, opens the windows and goes back to the phone)

M: Wait, I had underlined a sentence from a book. I want to read it to you. Here it is. Then. "These stony-hearted scoundrels, who by false flattery deceive innocent maidens and then abandon them to their fate, are nothing but cowards without honour. "

G: Thank you.

M: You're welcome. Wait, I have another one. "These petty exploiters, who with mellifluous words and vain promises circle only to gratify their lust, then vanish like smoke, nothing is but cowardly cowards." What do you think?

G: Well, they are not objectionable. But there is always a reason...

(Maria Elisa jerks up and rages at Giorgio).

M: What? What did you say? Are you saying that you had a good reason for treating those poor girls as a piece of garbage, not to say worse?

G: No, no. You didn't understand that.

M: Let's see if you understand it. When we met, you were always kind, considerate and gallant. Exactly as you had been with Maddalena and the others. I know because, unfortunately, you weren't even very smart; you picked them all in the same circle. When I got involved with you, I was warned. And it went as they said. Then you fell in love, and that changed everything.

G: Bitches...

M: You still don't understand that you were the asshole? Do you still continue to justify your behaviour? Do you know who wrote those sentences?

G: No. A Tuscan artist?

M: A Londoner from Naples, a certain Pascal de Napoli.

G: Ah.

M: Yeah, just Ah. Giorgio, I don't believe half a word you're saying. Antonio wrote a whole book condemning violence and exploitation of men, women and children, especially. It was one of the first books he wrote. He was young, and he didn't have any success until he became an established one for other, less profound books. So, for you to tell me that Antonio was laughing at your prey, it's no use. It's all lies. Do you know what you're doing?

G: What?

M: You are confessing part of the sin and also absolving yourself. You are worthless. I hope Antonio has written a book about your last meeting. If someone publishes it, I'll buy a hundred copies and distribute them around the neighbourhood. You really are a quarter of a man.

G: I didn't know you collected Pascal de Napoli's books.

M: Yes, I have them in English, too, for that matter. But you don't know, I've been taking English lessons for years. Right?

G: No, not really.

M: Here you go, there is only you. No one else exists but you. That's your problem. You only think about your own shit. And you broke a friendship, and who knows how many other things, for the sake of a quiet life. You thought, nay, you say you were doing it for me. You always did everything just and exclusively for you.

G: I did everything for us! And to this day, I still think of you and the boys.

M: For goodness sake! Don't think about it! Keep thinking about yourself, and you might live a better life.

G: Now it turns out that Antonio was your ideal man. Maybe you even thought about him as a possible lover.

M: Don't be an asshole. I hid my admiration for Antonio because I didn't want to hurt you. I thought that, for some well-founded reason, he had broken the friendship with you. Instead, now we know it was you from the very beginning. The stories you told me were all half-truths or half-lies. See as it fits.

G: Would you have had sex with him, given the opportunity?

M: What kind of questions is that? According to you, a male-female relationship has to be only sexual? But according to you, people only seek gratification and fulfilment through sex? You are sick! Get treated!

G: Okay, okay. But isn't it true that you women feel attracted to powerful, charismatic men and so on?

M: You women. Like we're all the same. But hold on, do you think you represent the whole male human race? I hope not; otherwise, we are in trouble!

(Maria Elisa, laughing)

G: So you would have never slept with Antonio.

M: No.

(Giorgio feels a hot flush assaulting him).

G: Slut! Twice a slut, you are!

(Maria Elisa gets angry)

M: Ignorant little fucking soldier! How dare you? You are lucky we have two children together. Otherwise, I wouldn't talk to you anymore. Slut was your sister who had an affair with her married neighbour. Not me. The cuckold is her husband, who knew and said nothing. Ah, true, you men are all the same, all for the quiet living. How dare you?

G: I know you fucked Antonio! In Milan, at the Splendor!

M: You're so fucked up! I've never cheated on you! Never!

G: Antonio told me that!

M: What an asshole! I haven't seen Antonio since 92!

G: Antonio would never lie!

M: Then, if he never lied, it would have meant that you were ten times as shitty. Because you've been hinting to me all these years that he was a liar. You are the real liar. Now tell me straight what that dead asshole told you.

G: He told me that you fucked. He told me you went to the book signing, and then you fucked. But he didn't know who you were. You told him your name was Nina. He found out when we coincidentally talked about your book signing.

(Maria Elisa laughs, hysterical).

M: But I will put up a statue in his honour! This man was a genius, not just an author. You can tell from his books, for goodness sake! Pure genius! Great!

(Maria Elisa doesn't stop laughing while Giorgio gets angrier and angrier).

G: Are you mocking me too? Adding insult to injury!

M: Simpleton! You would have realised he was mocking you if you weren't so ignorant and bitter! What an idiot you are! And you kept this inside for months? Why? For the sake of a quiet life? But I'm coming to the funerals with you tomorrow! I have to kiss him on the lips before they bury him!

G: I don't understand. What's going on? Will you stop laughing and let me understand?

M: Wait, I have to go rinse my face. Oh God, what a laugh!

(Giorgio whispers, knowing that Maria Elisa is not on the phone)

G: But look at this bitch....

(Maria Elisa returns to the phone)

M: Sorry, but I couldn't control myself. Ooof! So I was in the office that evening, then dinner at the Splendor restaurant.

G: First, you were at Antonio's book signing.

M: But what book signing? What the fuck did I know about the signing. Maybe it's not even true that there was a signing; did you check?

G: Continue.

M: I stopped by the Galleria by the Duomo, then we went to dine with a colleague at Splendor, as I said before because Angelo told me I absolutely had to taste their Neapolitan cuisine. It was a Neapolitan week, and he wanted to thank me for helping him close an important deal with an Arab tycoon who was going to refurbish his yacht docked in Portofino. So we went there.

G: What about the dedication? Why did Antonio know what it said? Explain that to me. And then, the book? So many coincidences.

M: Angelo gave the book to me. He had read the reviews and knew that this book, originally in English, was written by this established Neapolitan author after a big sales success in London. So the book had come out a few days before. Angelo had read the English version of the book. In fact, he actually read all of Antonio's books. And he was an admirer of his. Think that, for obvious reasons, I didn't even tell him I knew him.

G: The dedication!

M: Of course, the dedication. You haven't read any of Antonio's books. In one book, Carmela's, an artist talks to her and says, "Dearest, you could have been the muse I didn't know I was looking for", or something like that. So Angelo took a sentence from that book to thank me for the help I gave him on the project. What did he say my name was? Antonio, I mean.

G: Nina.

M: That's a nice name. Nina—the English book on fairy tales includes a fairy tale about a little girl who is an unsuspecting girl. Nina, that's right. When you come home, I'll give it to you, so you might learn something!

(Maria Elisa laughs out loud).

G: This son of a bitch! He was dying, and he took the piss out of me! What an embarrassment. They all know you betrayed me with him! There was such a crowd…

M: They must have spent days at the Lotto teller.

G: But they will not win, anyway, since it's a lie.

(They both laugh)

G: You're right. Why did he do that?

M: Because he wanted to piss you off. He wanted you to get out of your comfort zone. He wanted you to feel some emotion, maybe. I don't think he did it to make you fight with me. In fact, he did it knowing that he was on the safe side because he knew that you wouldn't have said anything to me. And if it weren't for his death, you still wouldn't have said anything.

G: And me becoming an alcoholic because of him...

M: Whatever, him with cigarettes and you with alcohol. I can't believe it. What a prank he played on you...

G: That little shit!

M: Be glad you met him, at least. He was brilliant as a person. Ultimately, he came looking for you on purpose to Naples to say goodbye for the last time. If he didn't love you, he wouldn't have done that.

G: But no, he was there for a movie from one of his books that hadn't come out yet. That's what he told me.

M: Okay, I'll tell you something I should have told you, perhaps.

G: No, huh? What else I don't know.

M: Gennaro had sent me a message on Instagram two days before your meeting saying that Antonio was in Italy and he wanted to know where you were those days. I told him I would ask you, but he said no because Antonio wanted it to be a surprise. He also told me that a few years before, Antonio's father saw you by your building once and told you that Antonio was coming down to go the airport. You left so you wouldn't see him on purpose.

G: I don't remember.

M: Tell someone else these lies. You told me the same night.

G: Then it must have been true.

M: Of course, it was true. So what was I saying? Oh yes, he wanted to surprise you. I have to say I didn't know whether to tell him that you were in Napoli, but then I told myself it would be nice to meet you and maybe clear the air between you now that you are in your sixties.

G: So he came especially to Italy for me?

M: No, he was in Turin for a film. He travelled to Naples in the morning and had the plane in the early afternoon to see someone for casting.

G: So he lied to me.

M: But holy Mother of God, look on the bright side of it. A man terminally ill comes on purpose to see you because he wants to die peacefully with a clear conscience, and you think of the lie? You didn't understand shit, Giorgio. One friend you had, the only one who really loved you, and you pushed him away because you wanted to live quietly. That tranquillity that cost you everything. Friendship, family, affections, mental health... Giorgio, you're an idiot!

G: I'm sorry. I think I've ruined everything. I will do as you say. I will certainly seek help.

M: Now go to sleep. And apologise to me for doubting my fidelity. You are lucky that I still love you. Good night. And throw away the alcohol that doesn't suit you.

G: Good night. Forgive me, please. I have to start preparing for departure.

M: Bye.

(Maria Elisa walks around the room, still holding a cigarette. She ponders. Then she starts to cry. She picks up her cell phone and begins to write)

WhatsApp:

You: "Hello Angelo, I hope you are well. Tomorrow I would like to talk to you about something. Could you return me a favour? And urgently. If you can, browse on Google and search for Pascal de Napoli. If you go to Wikipedia, there is his complete bibliography. You may not need it, but I need an alibi for something that happened years ago that came up today. I'll call you in the morning. A kiss ."

Angelo Cipriani: "Hi Elisa, sure. For you, anything. I don't know who this Pascal is, but I'll look him up online. See you tomorrow. Kisses."

ACT THREE

(A man, Pascal de Napoli, sits behind a desk at a bookstore in Milan. The author talks about his latest book, The Ghosts of the Past, and speaks to those in attendance)

Pascal: This book draws inspiration from real events and people in my life, but each character is an amalgamation of at least three people I have met on my journey. I have let all the characters represent me. Human nature is complex and multifaceted, and in these pages, I do not intend to paint anyone as completely good or bad. All the protagonists, without antagonists, possess positive, negative traits, and reflect different shades of the human experience.

(Applause)

P: The events narrated have been fictionalised and dramatised to create the right atmosphere and emphasise universal themes. This is a story about people, their weaknesses, and their humanity. People who, despite their differences, share the same basic needs.

(Applause continues)

(Pascal talks to the people in the queue, signs the books, and is congratulated and thanked)

(A woman approaches and hands him the book. She says nothing. As Pascal tries to sign it, she nets his hand on the book)

Maria Elisa: No, thank you, I don't want a signature. Do you recognise me? Antonio?

Pascal/Antonio: Not really. Should I?

M: We have only seen each other twice, but your presence in my life has been constant. Even before we met.

A: I'm sorry, but I don't remember you.

(Antonio looks around as if seeking rescue. Many thoughts pass through his mind.)

A: What do you want from me? I really don't remember.

M: I'll help you, then. I'm Elisa.

A: Ah! Giorgio's wife! Hi Elisa. Sorry, I thought it was somewhat psycho, obsessed with me. There are some around.

M: Don't flatter yourself?

A: I don't flatter myself so easily, but I think it's a natural instinct when someone tells you they've known you since before they met you. Anyway, how are you?

(People in the queue murmur. Antonio raises his hand to apologise for the delay.)

A: Elisa, can I continue to meet readers? If you have time, we can talk in fifteen minutes when I finish. What do you say? Is that okay?

M: Sorry, I didn't mean to interrupt your meeting.

A: Thank you.

(Antonio continues to exchange greetings, compliments and thanks with readers)

A: Elisa. Come on. Let's have a coffee if you can.

M: With pleasure.

(*Antonio greets the bookstore staff and walks, with Maria Elisa at his side, to the first cafe in the Galleria with tables outside.*)

A: Please, is it okay here?

(*Maria Elisa nods and places her bag on a chair beside the one she has chosen.*)

A: What will you have?

M: A coffee for me. Thank you.

A: Boy! Would you bring a coffee and an aperitif? An Aperol Spritz. Thank you.

M: Do you come to Milan often?

A: Not really. I've been missing from this place for years. But it's nice to come back. I don't have great memories of this city, but it has changed a lot since the nineties or eighties.

M: Yes, I read something about your years in Milan. It must have been tough for a young Southerner with the Lombard League around.

A: In fact, it wasn't. It was like England today. Foreigners are not well-liked. The difference was that I wasn't a foreigner here, at least according to the Constitution of the Italian Republic.

M: Now it's quite different. I've had to get used to it, too, though.

A: I see you have settled in well. You have completely lost the accent.

M: I took diction classes. They were helpful. You also have a different accent.

A: Wait until I drink a little, and you'll see!

M: In vino veritas.

A: Absolutely. Tell me, how is Giorgio doing?

M: You know, he's always fine. He doesn't look around much. As long as he's fine, he thinks everybody's fine.

A: He's always been like that. It was his way of not looking inside himself.

M: So true. He didn't have a personal growth path. The work doesn't help. If you ask him what he does at work, he doesn't answer.

A: Like the child in the commercial who climbs, plays, and studies, when he comes home, he tells his mother he didn't do anything special.

(Antonio laughs)

M: But in his case, I think he doesn't really do anything.

A: Poor Italy.

M: Yeah.

A: I know you have two children?

M: Yes, they are my, our joy. Both healthy and very active with sports and music. In short, they are different from their father.

A: More like the mother?

M: I would not say so. I was locked in the house all day as a child. My father was distrustful of everything and everyone. The priests were paedophiles, the instructors sex maniacs, the neighbours pigs. And my sisters and I could do very little on our own. At least I was studying, though.

A: And may I ask, what did you study? I don't think I ever knew.

M: Architecture. I graduated with my first child already in school. But I made it. Now, I work for a very important firm.

A: Congratulations.

M: Thank you. On the other hand, am I wrong, or have you never graduated?

A: You are not wrong.

M: Yet you became famous. Writer, politician, journalist and many other things.

A: Let's say I was lucky

M: Here's the Neapolitan who pops up.

A: But no, in life, you need luck. To be in the right place at the right time, for example.

M: You've been in so many places at the right time.

A: Eh, yes. Always fidgety. I can't sit still, ergo.

M: Better than spending your whole life in an office behind a desk waiting for a paycheck.

A: Who knows. I know many people living happily like that. People who succeed in other fields outside of work. After all, even I spend months inside a studio writing.

M: I've always wondered how long it takes to write a book. How long does it take?

A: It depends on the books. This book was an example of celerity. Three weeks, four hours a week. From the idea to the final revision. Then, it takes three months to publish, but I am not usually the one that handles that.

M: Man! Unbelievable.

A: But the drinks? It's like Naples, rather than Milan.

M: They *Terronised* themselves instead of Italianising us.

A: Apparently, they have. Here are the drinks.

M: So Cheers!

A: *Addo' va!* Here's to friendships that were never born and those that died. But especially to unexpected encounters.

M: Yay! In one sentence, you've already addressed three themes you'll want to discuss, maybe for the next book.

(Antonio laughs)

A: In the book you have in your bag, there is already everything we discussed and will be discussing.

M: Even clairvoyant!

A: No, that book is me wanting to come to terms with the past. So you will find this kind of talk.

M: And how do you see the future?

A: Always in retrospect. For me, the future is the past coming back. I have reached a state where I am more fascinated to know how they lived in the Middle Ages than how my grandchildren will live. And the same for my life. For me, it's all one continuous past. You speak English. So you understand what I mean.

M: So only the past and the present matter to you?

A: Not exactly. About the future, I don't worry. I can't imagine it.

M: With the imagination you have, it's hard to believe.

A: All my books speak in the past or present. Even when situations take place in the future, I make them develop in the present tense.

M: As with "Vite a Meta'."

A: Yes, I was thinking of that as an example.

M: That's one of my favourite books of yours.

A: For me as well. Although I always think the one I'm writing will be my favourite. Kind of like children. The first gives unexplainable emotions, but the last you get attached to differently, with a different eye. I don't know what thirds are like, much less will you be able to tell me.

(Moment of silence)

A: So? Elisa, what do we do here?

M: It's not easy to explain.

A: Let's try. Some cues I gave you earlier. Let's talk about Giorgio, our friendship and its end, or this encounter?

M: Let's leave my husband out of this. You know him well. Maybe better than I do.

A: I doubt I ever knew him. Continue sorry.

M: Let's talk about you and me.

A: Meaning, I talk to you about me, and you talk to me about you? I don't think it's possible to discuss Us. There's never been an us. You've been engaged to my best friend for years, and I'd never met you.

M: Exactly. Why?

A: You should be the last person to ask.

M: Giorgio told me I wasn't the right woman for him, according to you.

A: I have to be honest, but I don't think any woman is right for Giorgio because Giorgio is not right for any woman. But I don't think I ever said anything like that. When I came back from abroad, Giorgio always found excuses on your behalf not to meet us. Then, I stopped even asking for it. Then he took care of it and stopped seeing me, too.

M: What did you do to him?

A: I guess nothing. Giorgio just disappeared all of a sudden.

M: So you thought it was my fault.

A: No, I thought you didn't feel like Giorgio and I would be continuing our friendship, and when you said no to being my witness, I knew it was over.

M: Didn't Giorgio tell you the reason for my refusal?

A: No, I don't think we saw or heard from each other many times after my matrimony, so we never had the opportunity to discuss it.

M: I had some big family problems with my mother; she would later die taking her life.

A: I'm sorry. I didn't know that. Condolence.

M: It's history. She suffered a lot. She stopped that day in November.

A: I see. And why couldn't you be my witnesses? You came to the wedding anyway. You didn't have to arrange it, did you?

M: I wasn't in the right frame of mind then. On the other hand, you were in Australia when we married.

A: Yes, I was sorry, but I couldn't come over for a day.

M: I don't know if my husband ever thanked you. In case I do now.

A: You're welcome. So, if it wasn't you or me who wanted to break the friendship, that leaves only one possible culprit.

M: Yes, he still can't have stable friendships to this day.

A: Neither do I. The friendship with Giorgio was the last real friendship. I backed away from any timid attempt at anything looking more than an acquaintance. I got burned. And I still don't know why. Maybe one day I will know. In truth, I doubt it, but never despair.

M: Could it all have been a misunderstanding?

A: I don't think so. Friends talk to each other, argue, clarify. We didn't do any of the three. The last time I tried was in 2000; he said he couldn't see me. He was busy.

M: I didn't know that.

A: I'm surprised. I was convinced that you didn't want to deal with me, I must admit.

M: No, absolutely not. I was pissed at my father-in-law belittling my husband by exalting you. But I knew very well that you and my then-boyfriend were completely different. Honestly, I liked him. I liked his goliardic ways, his being a man with his weaknesses and insecurities, which you didn't seem to have.

A: Far from not having them! I flaunted fake confidence, but not with Giorgio; he knew everything about me. Even today, I have few certainties and am always questioning myself. Why do you think I have so many interests? I haven't figured out what I will be when I grow up.

M: Hard to believe that.

A: I assure you. He who has certainties in life settles down. I never did.

M: So, you're telling me Giorgio is a secure guy?

A: No, Giorgio is a guy who absorbs security from others because he doesn't have any of his own. Sorry, Elisa, weren't we supposed to talk about something else?

M: Yes, let's talk about why I'm here.

(Finishes coffee)

M: I think sparkling wine suits us best.

A: I would say a champagne is more suitable.

M: Champagne, to toast an unexpected and pleasant encounter...

A: A bottle of Veuve Clicquot, please. So tell me why you are here.

M: First of all, I wanted to see you to tell you that I'm a fan.

A: Mine or Pascal's?

M: I understand the difference. Then let's say Pascal's.

A: Okay.

M: Then I wanted to see you again because you remained a question mark in my imagination. Sort of a dividing element. If you were a politician, I would compare you to Berlusconi. Some hated him, some who loved him.

A: And which side are you on?

M: I'm trying to figure that out. Although I know that a quick meeting will not resolve the issue.

A: The meeting can always be extended if you are not hurrying to go back home.

M: Are you flirting with me?

A: Actually, yes. I'm trying to take you to dinner because, still, I wouldn't say I like to eat alone after so many years, especially if I go to good restaurants.

M: I think I can accept the invitation. Where would you take me?

A: It depends on your opinion of me.

(They laugh with complicity)

M: So far, I have to agree with my father-in-law. Unfortunately.

A: That's a good thing. Continue.

M: In your books, I often find points of view dissonant from common feeling. Do you do this because you are convinced or to create discussions or arguments?

A: I'll answer you with a question. Do you think that a man, straight, in a Christian country like Italy decides to complicate his life by choosing to be gay?

M: No, I think it's natural. Isn't it?

A: Of course. Do you think I should decide to write against the most widespread sentiment to be targeted in the press, on the street, and so on? I would be masochistic. And I assure you I have a very low pain threshold.

M: So you think your positions about the Church, sexuality, animal rights, and immigrants are contrary to common sentiment?

A: Yes. Is your husband still anti-gay? He used to call them *gayants* to indicate their attitude rather than their status?

M: He seems to have calmed down recently but remains convinced it is a fad. And as such, it will pass.

A: Great. That's something already. When I was young, Giorgio hated them. What else do you want to know about me?

M: Who is Pascal?

A: Pascal is someone who doesn't like to compromise. Someone who started writing about too-serious topics and then melted into the ordinary, writing dialogue books that ordinary people have no trouble understanding. He writes stories that everyone could write. Do you know when you read about a new invention and say I could have invented it? Pascal is the one who invented hot water.

M: So you minimise yourself.

A: Far from it. I think it's brilliant. Building popularity for the Lapalissian is genius. Antonio would never have succeeded. My first books? Nobody read them. The rewritten fairy tales and the books about the condition of women were Antonio's books. They were either too trivial or too challenging.

M: I like your early books.

A: But you like them now because you know who Pascal is. Until the book with Carmela as a protagonist, I had sold about 20 copies of each book. Now you can't find them anymore.

M: What is there about you in your books?

A: Everything. As I said tonight at the book presentation, I'm everywhere, in every character.

M: So you don't have a well-defined personality?

A: Of course I do. And that's what creates bewilderment and a sense of insecurity in the readers. I identify with many people with contradictory traits. Are you always consistent?

M: No, on the contrary. I'm here tonight. More inconsistent than this...

A: Where is the inconsistency.

M: If Giorgio had done such a thing with a friend of mine, I would cut off his balls.

A: But I am not a friend of Giorgio. You came to meet Pascal or maybe the adult version of Antonio.

M: That's true. Nice champagne, by the way.

A: Cheers. To Pascal, to Antonio and especially to Elisa.

M: Cheers. And where do you put your wife?

A: She's at home. I guess she's fine.

M: Considering that you are a personality, your phone seems too quiet.

A: I keep it off most of the time.

M: What if your wife needs it?

A: I could do very little from Milan. She will call someone closer.

M: That is also true. Isn't she jealous?

A: No, we have no reason to be jealous. We are always very honest with each other.

M: So, will you tell her about this meeting?

A: If she asks what I did in Milan tonight, certainly.

M: Does she know us? I mean me and Giorgio by hearsay.

A: No. She knows I have old friends in Italy but doesn't know anything about them. About you guys, neither.

M: I would be jealous.

A: Are you jealous of your husband?

M: Jealous of Giorgio?

A: I think that's his name.

(Maria Elisa laughs)

M: No. I wish he would go out once in a while. He's like his father; he's obsessive with us.

A: So he must be in pain now.

M: No, he knows I'm at the office till late.

(They drink another flute of champagne each, all in one gulp, and refill two more flutes)

M: So if you cheated on your wife tonight, you would tell her?

A: If she asked me what I did tonight, yes.

M: You're kidding, right?

A: Sure.

(Maria Elisa laughs)

M: What a moron! I wonder how many lies you're telling me?

A: Enough to make you go to dinner with me.

M: I've already said yes.

A: Fuck! That's true! Come on, let's start again, I forgot.

(They both laugh)

M: If I don't like what you say, I can change my mind.

A: Then no. I'll confirm everything I've said so far.

(Pause for silence)

A: Tell me, are you faithful?

M: I was expecting this question.

A: I wonder why, eh?

M: Then I will answer by saying that I am not unfaithful. But until now, I have never had a chance to test my faithfulness.

A: Honest as an answer. So there is some hope.

M: Nice friendship you and Giorgio must have had. I didn't make you such a chuck.

A: I'm not, or I should say I wasn't.

M: So there's hope that Giorgio will become a little more like you were since you're becoming like him.

A: Becoming? I've been like him for years. But at least I'm not promising eternal love to anyone.

M: And your wife doesn't suspect?

A: My wife has no interest in suspecting. We are much more than lovers. We are accomplices. We are friends.

M: Watch out, you'll ditch your second marriage, too.

A: Tough luck, we'll make a third.

(They both laugh lightly)

M: What a philosophy you follow. Anyway, it aligns with the personages in the books.

A: I told you it's always me, everywhere, in every role.

M: So if you authored a book about me, I would be you and not me?

A: Who knows, maybe not. You're making me think now. Almost a muse you're becoming tonight.

M: Wow, what an honour!

A: Well, yes. I'm getting intrigued by the conversation. What a fortunate man my friend is.

M: Oh yeah, we mostly talk about money, what we've done during the day and what there is to eat. It's boring like hell.

A: And is that enough for you?

M: No, of course not. I would like more. I want a lot more. Oh God, the alcohol speaks.

A: Go let it talk; it intrigues me.

M: Is that because I am your friend's wife?

A: No, because I'm intrigued by people in general. But you have something that intrigues me more, maybe because I've always considered you, idealised you, as a monster.

M: Same for me. The fact that Giorgio was the only source of truth about the two of us must have created this distortion of personalities.

A: The bottle is empty. Shall we go to the restaurant I was telling you about?

M: Yes, where is it?

A: It's in the Brera quarter.

M: Do you mind if we go to a place I know? They have Neapolitan cuisine this week.

A: Sure, I like the idea. Walk or cab?

M: It's raining, cab, I would say. Okay?

(Antonio pays the bill, helps Maria Elisa put on her coat, and they walk to the cab stand. Without speaking)

M: Corso Vercelli, Splendor.

(Taxi driver hints that he knows the place and leaves).

(Neither of the two says a word. As if they were afraid that a third person might steal their conversation)

M: Here we go. Have you ever been here?

A: No, never. I usually stay towards the Duomo or towards Forlanini, close to the airport.

M: It's a nice hotel, but they also cook well.

A: We'll see.

(Maria Elisa asks for a table for two, preferably away from the walking path. The waiter accommodates her request.)

A: Nice restaurant. Good choice.

M: They do a Neapolitan week from time to time. I came here with my colleagues.

A: Champagne? I wouldn't want to mix alcohol.

M: But do you pay, or do they reimburse your expenses?

A: You readers pay for it.

M: Ah, that's okay then. I am getting back the 12 euros I paid for the book.

(The two order champagne and the set menu, typical of the soiree's menu)

A: Great! We don't have to choose.

M: Well, yes, otherwise, we would have eaten around midnight. I am a picky chooser.

A: Enjoy your meal.

(*The discussion stops. There is a feeling of tension. Not a negative tension, though*)

A: Elisa.

M: Antonio.

A: I want to make love to you.

(*Maria Elisa gets embarrassed*)

M: So do I. But I don't know if it's the right thing.

A: Maybe it's not, but I want you.

M: Don't you think about Giorgio?

A: Can I think about that later?

(*Maria Elisa laughs*)

M: What a jerk. Your best friend.

A: Giorgio is not my friend. And he never was. I wonder if he is still your husband.

M: Not for long. What did you figure that out from?

A: You came to meet me. I don't see any other reason. Are you trying to decide, or have you already decided? Is there another man?

M: No. Actually, there is someone I like. But I don't think I could live with him.

A: Why not?

M: I don't know. There is something that stops me.

A: Then let him go.

M: He is a colleague of mine. His name is Angelo. And he is really an angel, but I feel the need to have a real man by my side. Not a jerk, but not a super corny one either. Do you understand what I mean?

A: Perfectly. I don't want to sound immodest, but I must deal with my boring fans. I am attracted only to women with strong personalities. You are one of the few. I could even write a book about you.

M: What a flatterer! I didn't think you were like that. Maybe you say it to get me into bed.

A: Even to get you into bed.

(Sighs, Maria Elisa)

M: Now I'm really turned on.

A: Let's go to my hotel.

M: Why not here?

A: Wait, I'll see if they have a room.

M: Are the readers still paying?

A: Of course they are.

M: You will definitely write a book after tonight, anyway. So I won't feel guilty for making you spend so much.

A: Fuck the money!

(He goes toward the hotel reception. Five minutes pass. He returns with an electronic card in his hand)

A: Are you ready?

M: Ready? I was when I heard you talk about your book. Now I'm way past that. If you don't take me to the room, I'm going to fuck you here.

A: Let's go then.

(Hand in hand, they walk to the elevator after crossing the entire restaurant, with her head on his shoulder)

M: Where is the elevator? Why is it taking so long?

A: Do we do it here?

M: What floor are we on?

A: Top one. Suite.

M: You're crazy! It will be 300 euros.

A: 500, to be exact, with a bottle of champagne included and breakfast, which we will not consume.

M: You are right.

A: That's all right.

(They arrive at the room. He opens, she enters, throws her shoes in the air, crosses the hall, and heads for the bedroom. He follows her.)

A: The champagne is coming soon.

M: I don't give a damn about the champagne. Come over here. Let me unbutton your pants.

A: Here I am.

(He approaches her, sitting on the bed.

He stands.

She unbuttons his pants.

He pulls down the zipper.

He starts panting. She stands up.

She throws him on the bed.

He pulls her to him to kiss her.

She lets him take her.

He pushes her down on her stomach and begins to pull up her skirt.

She turns around.

She pushes him down.

She signals for him to lie on his back.

The scene continues until both are exhausted.

They are lying next to each other, looking at the ceiling).

A: Wow.

M: Yes, Wow.

A: I never thought I would have had such an evening this morning.

M: Neither did I. I thought I would come and see you. From a distance and go away.

A: Then what happened?

M: What do I know? As soon as I heard you speak, I said to myself. What a man.

A: Well, not so much.

M: Giorgio is not your friend. I should be the one feeling guilty. Instead, I only feel guilty for being together for so many years.

A: Maybe you can make things right. Who knows?

M: I'll certainly fix them for me.

A: Are you going to leave him?

M: Until this morning, it was almost a forbidden wish. I've gone beyond it and realised it's what I want. The only forbidden thing is to stay with him.

A: Think about the children, too.

M: They are grown up. They will understand. Excuse me, but weren't you a heavy smoker?

A: Yes. I still am.

M: You didn't smoke the whole evening.

A: Well, I had the adrenaline pumping, not to mention the hormones. I need a cigarette now, though.

(*Antonio gets up naked, without covering himself, and takes two cigarettes from the packet. He lights them and gives one to Maria Elisa*)

M: I haven't had a cigarette in years.

A: Unfortunately, picking the habit back only takes a puff. I quit once for years, then started again as if I had never quit. I know they will be the ones to kill me.

M: Is it okay if I put on some music?

A: Yes, with pleasure.

M: Do you like Nina Simone?

A: Very much.

(Maria Elisa turns on her cell phone).

M: Shall we dance?

A: In the nude?

M: Why not. Maybe we'll get the urge back.

A: It never went away.

(They get up and start dancing to the notes of "I put a spell on you")

(They kiss)

M: Do you feel like going back to bed?

A: Very much so.

M: Let's do it then before we say goodbye.

(They start making love again.

This time, it's love.

Not sex, not passion.

Their intertwining bodies are like eddies in a rushing river.

The caresses are like light breezes caressing the skin.

The kisses are like flowers blooming, releasing precious nectar.

Their lovemaking is like dancing to music that only they can hear.

Ecstasy is a wave that sweeps over them, leaving them breathless.

The moans and sighs are the song of ancient sirens hovering in the air.

The sheets caress their skin like fine silks. Then, it all ends.)

M: Unfortunately, I have to go. Are you coming with me or are you staying here longer?

A: There's a bottle of champagne to finish. It's still outside the door. Would you like to drink some?

M: No, I have to go. Would you see me again?

A: Definitely.

M: I wouldn't. I think tomorrow I will consider tonight the biggest mistake of my life.

A: Not tonight, right?

M: No, definitely not.

(They kiss again. They look at each other, knowing they will never see each other again.)

A: I'm staying here tonight. Tomorrow morning, I'll go back to the hotel and pack. I have a plane to Paris at two o'clock.

M: Other city, other signatures, other women.

A: No, Paris is not for work. I am seeing a specialist for an assessment.

M: Are you unwell?

A: Yes. Years ago, they found a tumour in my lungs. They managed to save most of the right lung. But it seems to be back, more pissed off than before. You're the only person in the world who knows.

M: I'm sorry.

A: I'll give it a hard time before it wins.

M: I'll get ready now.

A: Taking a shower?

M: No, I'd better go; it's getting late.

A: Okay. It was nice making love to you. But it is even nicer to have met you and understand that you did not break my friendship with Giorgio. It's an epiphany for me. Thank you.

M: Wait. Can you write a dedication on the book?

A: With pleasure.

M: However, don't sign it as Pascal or Antonio. You were the first man who fascinated me and made me feel like a woman. Sign with a beautiful A. The first letter of the alphabet.

A: I hope you'll find a B soon.

(Laughter)

(Antonio writes the dedication)

M: Thank you. And it's beautiful. I will keep it forever in my memories. And even though I haven't read this book, it will become my favourite. Also because, you told me, it's also about me.

(Laughter)

M: Even if only for one evening, Antonio, I want to tell you... I know it sounds silly, but ... I love you, Pascal. I loved you tonight. Tomorrow, everything will be different.

A: I love you too, Nina. And tomorrow, I will still love you.

ACKNOWLEDGEMENT

Dear friends,

I would like to thank all of you who supported me and helped me in writing my book "The Ghosts of the Past".
In particular, special thanks to Luca Buonanno, aka Cognac, Marco Grimaldi, aka Big Brother, and Andrea Vestita for supporting me during the writing of the original version of this book.
Having you by my side on this journey was fundamental. Your friendship and support have been a priceless gift to me.
I hope that when you read the finished novel, you will recognise yourself in it and will be proud to have accompanied me on this adventure.

Thank you very much, my friends!

Luigi P

ABOUT THE AUTHOR

Luigi Pascal Rondanini (Aka Pascal De Napoli)

Luigi Pascal Rondanini's determination and tenacity in pursuing his ideals pushed him to leave his native Naples to pursue the opportunities offered by the world.

Born in November 1967 and raised in the capital of Campania, from a young age he cultivated a passion for writing and politics. The desire for social justice led him to actively engage in social issues and to write literary works inspired by these values.

At a very young age, he moved abroad to the United Kingdom, where he embarked on a brilliant career in the financial sector and continued his passion for writing, infusing his works with social and political themes with courage and frankness.

Despite living in London, Rondanini has never lost the connection with his Neapolitan roots after having lived on five continents. In his writings, Neapolitan culture and identity emerge vividly as an example of cultural diversity that enriches humanity.

Rondanini wants to inspire readers to pursue their dreams with courage and determination. His story demonstrates how, with commitment and sacrifice, you can achieve great goals while remaining true to yourself and your values.

BOOKS BY THIS AUTHOR

Vanished Echoes - A Breaking News Story

When a 10-year-old girl goes missing on her walk home from school, it sparks a rapidly escalating crisis told through the lens of an urgent primetime breaking news broadcast.

This gripping page-turner places you directly inside a marathon live telecast tracking each new development as it happens. Told in real-time through on-scene reports, profiling experts and official statements, this present-tense account builds nonstop suspense surrounding the girl's unknown fate over several frantic nights.

More than just a crime drama, Vanished Echoes weaves incisive social commentary on prejudice, mental health neglect and media power into the unfolding mystery. An inventive book that achieves what few works have dared – putting the reader at the heart of the story as virtual viewer.

I Fantasmi Del Passato (Versione Italiana)

In un bar alla periferia di Napoli, Antonio incontra casualmente il suo vecchio amico Giorgio, con cui non parlava da decenni. I due decidono di trascorrere la giornata insieme, tra ricordi e confessioni, in un viaggio nei meandri più reconditi delle loro esistenze e del loro turbolento passato. Antonio e Giorgio rievocano gli anni dell'adolescenza, quando la loro amicizia era stata improvvisamente interrotta senza un motivo apparente. Ripercorrono le scelte e i percorsi di vita che li hanno portati lontano l'uno dall'altro. Affrontano vecchi rancori, gelosie, incomprensioni.

The Tales To Grow By Collection: Tales To Grow By, A Whale's Mercy And Light Within In One Inspirational Volume

This collection of short stories aims to instill important life lessons in young readers through imaginative tales exploring friendship, courage, compassion, and personal growth.

Overall, these imaginative narratives subtly impart values of empathy, integrity, generosity, and compassion through archetypal characters and whimsical adventures. The collection aims to nurture wisdom and character in young readers.

Printed in Great Britain
by Amazon